Max Elliot Anderson

Terror at Wolf Lake

Tweener Press

Grand Haven, Michigan

Terror at Wolf Lake
By Max Elliot Anderson

Printed in the United States of America
Cover Art: Paul S. Trittin
Cover Photography: David Alan Wolters

Published by Tweener Press Division
Baker Trittin Concepts
P.O. Box 20
Grand Haven, Michigan 49417

To order additional copies please call (616) 846-8550
or email info@btconcepts.com
http://www.gospelstoryteller.com

Publishers Cataloging-Publication Data
Anderson, Max Elliot
        Terror at Wolf Lake - Tweener Press Adventure
        Series / Max Elliot Anderson - Grand Haven,
        Michigan: Baker Trittin Concepts, 2004

                p.   cm.

Library of Congress Control Number: 2003112229
        ISBN: 0-9729256-6-X
        1. Juvenile   2. Fiction   3. Religious   4. Christian
        I. Title   II. Terror at Wolf Lake
JUV033010

Dedicated

to

Jim and Sarah,

the best listening ears

a storyteller could imagine.

Chapter 1

Eddy Thompson was known by his friends and his enemies for one thing. Eddy cheated . . . and not just sometimes. He cheated on anything, anytime, anywhere. At the same time, he was pretty slick about it. People around Eddy knew when he was up to something, but they could seldom actually catch him.

"If you don't change your ways," his principal at school warned him one day, "you can plan to spend the rest of your life in prison." Not the kind of encouragement an ordinary twelve-year-old student needs to hear. But then, Eddy wasn't exactly ordinary. He'd already been to court and nearly got shipped off to juvenile detention twice.

Eddy's squinting eyes, dark slick hair, and pointed features did nothing to lessen his shifty reputation.

"It's easier to ask forgiveness than permission," he'd say. "That's my motto."

"You have a very sharp mind," a teacher once

complimented. "There's no telling how far you could go if you put it to doing the right things." But Eddy tended to ignore such comments.

Eddy lived in Crown Point, Indiana. The town is famous as the place where the FBI brought one of the worst gangsters in American history for trial. His name was John Dillenger. Eddy liked the idea that this criminal also grew up in Indiana.

"Best thing to ever come out of this state," he liked to say about Dillenger.

John Dillenger robbed banks.

At least Eddy hadn't gone that far yet. But he'd done his share of stealing from stores in the area . . . more than his share actually.

"People who pay retail are stupid," he'd say.

The way Eddy figured it, he had a good excuse for the way he acted. "Everything I know about beating the system I learned from my dad," he'd announce proudly. "And he's never even been arrested."

You could say that Eddy took dishonesty to a whole new level. If it were possible for a student to major in the subject of cheating, Eddy could probably teach the class. He'd definitely get straight A's and find his name at the top of the principal's list. He was on a list all right, but not for his good grades.

This was the last class period before Christmas break. Weather forecasters predicted a colder than normal winter. So far they had been right on target. Heavy snow already covered the ground. The temperatures and wind-chill readings had been brutal.

If Eddy didn't get a B or better on the exam this afternoon, he was going to flunk history. If that happened, he was in danger of being held back a year. This thought alone left him feeling colder than anything winter could threaten.

"That's just not gonna happen," he told his friends defiantly as he snapped a pencil right in half.

"Only because part of the test is about your hero," Chet teased.

Although Chet always did his best to follow the rules, he was probably Eddy's best friend. Eddy watched him constantly. "How come you're so different?" he asked Chet one day.

"It's something on the inside. I'll tell you about it sometime."

Then there was Rusty Arnold. It was difficult to decide what Rusty did best . . . complain or worry. He and Chet were best friends and went to the same church.

Chet and Rusty liked Eddy a lot. When he wasn't cheating, he was fun to be around. They only wished he'd change the way he did things.

"Yeah," Rusty added, "you should ace the Dillenger questions."

"I know he was smart enough to break out of our jail even when everybody said that'd be impossible."

"He was smart all right," Chet said, "but not smart enough."

"What do you mean?" Eddy asked.

"You must not have read the whole chapter. The guy *got it* on a street in Chicago."

"That's because he messed up," Eddy answered. "I don't intend to let that happen. I'm gettin' an A on the test and that's that."

"This I gotta see," Rusty challenged.

Eddy looked around. "I have a secret weapon," he told them quietly.

"What is it *this* time?" Chet asked.

"Last night I went over to the apartments where our teacher lives."

"What did you do? Get down on your knees, pound on the door, and beg her for extra credit?" Chet teased.

"Better!"

"Better than extra credit?" Rusty asked.

"I did a little dumpster diving."

"Huh?"

"Dumpster diving. You know. I went through her trash and guess what I found?"

"Trash most likely."

"Yeah, that too. But I also found three crinkled up papers with all the answers on them."

"You did?"

"Sure. Want to see them?"

Chet held up his hands. "No way. I studied all week for this test. I'm not taking any chances."

"Whatever you say," Eddy sneered.

Just then the bell rang. Chet, Eddy, and Rusty joined the rest of their friends in Mrs. Hokstra's history class.

A half hour later, Eddy was the first one finished. He stood up and marched proudly to the front of the class where he dropped his exam on the desk.

"Finished so soon?" his teacher asked.

"It was simple," he told her.

"We'll see," she responded.

As Eddy headed for the door an uneasy feeling came over him. *Exactly what did she mean by that,* he wondered? He shuffled to the school library and waited while his friends finished their tests. Eddy sat there all alone until the bell sounded. Soon Chet and Rusty came to the door.

"You going to spend your Christmas break in here, or shall we go home now?" Rusty asked.

Eddy shuddered. "Don't even think such a horrible thought. Actually I wanted to ask you guys about something."

"What?" Chet asked.

"Well, you know my dad owns a cabin on Wolf Lake, up in Michigan?"

"Yeah, so?"

"So he was talking about going up there between Christmas and New Year's."

"Whatever for?" Rusty asked. "I thought your cabin was only for . . . like . . . spring and summer."

"It is, but we have a fireplace and a stove. It'd be cold, but us guys could handle it."

"Us guys?" Chet asked.

"He wants you both to come with us. Your dads, too."

"What is there to do up there?" Rusty asked.

"Lots of fun stuff."

"Name one."

"One? I can give you a bunch of them. People go ice fishing on the lake up there."

"Do they catch any ice?" Rusty joked.

"You've never been ice fishing, Russ?"

"Never."

"I think you'd like it. Plus our cabin is in the middle of nowhere. Who knows what might happen in a deserted place like that? You've never seen dark like it is up there at night."

"I don't think I like the sound of that," Rusty warned.

"Me neither," Chet added.

"Our dads will be there, too. Come on. What could possibly happen to us?"

Chapter 2

When Eddy came home from school, his father was already there.

"Hey, Dad, I thought you were supposed to be at work."

"I called in sick."

"What's wrong?"

"Nothing. I did it so we could get some things together for the cabin. Your friends coming?"

"I don't know yet." Eddy went to the computer, brought up his buddy list, clicked on his friend's screen names, and IMed Rusty and Chet.

"So can you come?" he wrote.

"I have to wait for my dad to get home from work," Rusty answered.

"I'll let you know after supper," Chet responded.

"If you guys don't wanna go," Eddy continued, "I'll just have to find someone who does."

Eddy switched off his computer. Deep down he wished he had parents like Rusty's and Chet's. His father didn't particularly care what he did. *Just once I'd like him to tell me when I did something wrong,* he thought.

Later that evening both of Eddy's friends called to say they could go to the cabin. Their dads said yes, too. The only thing left was to settle on the time. Over the next few days it was announced they would all ride together in a new Suburban Eddy's father had just brought home.

"I told the dealer I'd like to try it out for a few days, then make my decision," he told his son. "The truth is, I have no intention of buying a beast like that. But it'll be big enough to haul the bunch of us up there and back. Then I'll tell the dealer it wasn't quite what I had in mind."

Eddy thought that was pretty smart. Even smarter than when his mother went to an exclusive store, bought an expensive dress, wore it once to one of his dad's important parties, and then took it back to the store the next day for her money back because it didn't fit right.

In many ways Eddy didn't have a fighting chance at learning right from wrong. Well, he knew the difference. Something inside kept reminding him which was which, but he liked using his parents as an excuse to go right on cheating.

His whole family was like that. An older cousin went

from job to job. He'd sign up for a big bonus, work for a few months, and then look for another company that paid a bonus. Another cousin kept joining a DVD club. Each time he used a different name and one of his friend's addresses. So far, he was up to sixty-five movies.

The cabin trip was set to begin on December twenty-sixth. According to the plan, they would return before New Year's Eve. That was because Eddy's father had another important party to attend where he could impress a few of his clients. He also invited Chet's and Rusty's parents to go to the party with him.

Christmas was uneventful at Eddy's house this year except for the satellite TV system his father brought home. "We get to keep it for three months," he announced. "Then I'll tell the salesman it wasn't exactly what we wanted. All I have to do is keep going to different stores and we'll have free service for a whole year."

Eddy had already used the same scam on a couple music clubs, nearly doubling his CD collection for only a few cents. Like his cousin, he'd have them sent to friend's houses and keep changing his address on each order.

Finally, on the day after Christmas, Eddy and his father loaded the new Suburban with boxes filled with food, lots of warm clothes, boots, hats, gloves, and other supplies. It looked like they might be heading off to the North Pole, not a simple three-and-a-half-hour trip into Michigan.

They made the rounds to pick up the other four travelers. By eleven in the morning the adventurers were blasting down the interstate. The trip took them first around the southern tip of Lake Michigan. They continued driving up along the eastern shore of that great lake before turning inland.

"It looks even colder up here than back at home," Rusty commented.

"I don't think it's possible to be any colder than the winter we've already had," Rusty's father called back from the front seat.

But it was cold, deadly cold. Eddy and his friends looked out onto Lake Michigan where the wind and heavy waves had built giant ice formations far out into the water.

"Is it always frozen like that?" Chet asked.

"Not always," Eddy's father answered. "This winter is unusual."

Before long the boys fell asleep in the soft leather seats. About an hour later Eddy's father decided to stop for burgers at a place he liked. "They make them twice as thick as any of those other fast food joints," he said. He gave Eddy a twenty-dollar bill so he could buy lunch for himself and his friends.

Each boy ordered the captain's platter. It included a

gigantic double hamburger, big fries, an apple pie, and a large drink. The boys' meals came to a grand total of eighteen dollars and sixty-five cents with tax. When the girl behind the counter gave Eddy his change, she made a mistake . . . a big mistake!

After he and his friends sat down at their table, Eddy held out his hand. "Look at this," he smiled. "That dumb girl must have thought I gave her a fifty. She gave me back more change than the measly twenty I gave her."

"You have to give it back," Rusty challenged.

"Nothin' doin'! Her mistake . . . her loss. Besides, the owner looks like he makes plenty of money anyway. He can afford it."

Eddy's friends knew they should have done something. They felt uncomfortable not saying anything, but they just kept quiet. That's the way it was with most of the people in Eddy's life. No one ever did anything to try and turn him around.

The boys continued gulping their lunch as if nothing had happened. Before long the adventurers were back on the road. About an hour later they pulled off the Interstate onto a smaller road, and not long after that they were driving along a narrow road with tall pine trees on both sides. The farther they drove the more remote the area became.

Finally, their truck turned off onto a dirt road. Well, it looked like it might have been made of dirt, but right now, with all the snow, it was hard to tell for sure. What they *could* see is that this road was only wide enough for one car to travel on at a time.

"What's it like up here in the summer?" Chet asked.

"The trees are so full of leaves," Eddy's father began, "you can't see or hear anything. In fact, you wouldn't have any idea where our cabin sits if you didn't already know it was there."

"Isn't that kinda scary?" Rusty asked.

"Not really. In the summer there are lots of other people around here."

Chet broke in, "Yeah, but it isn't summer."

"That may be, but *nobody* comes up here in the winter. We should be perfectly safe."

"We're coming up," Rusty said.

Eddy kind of liked that his friends were afraid. He decided that as long as the dads were with them, they could take care of just about anything.

The truck came to an abrupt stop. "Is this as far as you can drive in?" Chet's father asked.

"No problem," Eddy's father answered. He'd told Eddy earlier that he picked out the most expensive Suburban he could find. He switched it to four-wheel drive, shifted into low gear, and began to push through the heavy drifts like a snowplow. Ten minutes later he announced, "There she is."

Everyone looked out to see a lonely isolated cabin sitting beneath towering oak and pine trees. There wasn't another cabin they could see in any direction. The place looked like one of the first pioneer settlements.

Everyone pitched in, quickly dragging things from the truck into the cabin. They found solid ice covering the inside of all the windows.

"You boys can start bringing in wood from the pile out back," Eddy's father instructed. "Soon as you do that, we'll get some heat going in this freezer."

The boys hurried to get that job done. Ever since stepping out of the warmth of the truck, they kept feeling colder by the second. The cabin had electricity but no running water. That came from a hand pump. There was only one bathroom, and this time of year they had to flush using a bucket full of water.

There were four bedrooms. Each dad chose one and the boys decided to stay together in the fourth.

A stone fireplace ran along one wall in the main room. The kitchen had a wood-burning stove they could use for cooking and heat. Over in a corner of the living room stood another wood-burning stove. That one was used only for heating.

"If we keep the fires burning," Eddy's father told them, "it won't matter how cold it gets outside. We should be fine in here."

While the boys gathered firewood, Rusty noticed a high wooden fence protecting three sides of the back yard.

"Why do you have such a huge fence?" he asked Eddy's father.

"We've had some problems with winter break-ins. That's one of the reasons I wanted to come here . . . to sort of check up on things. Right on the other side of that fence is another small access road. This is a pretty remote area. The police don't patrol out here after Labor Day. So it would be easy for someone to drive up to the back of our cabin on that hidden dirt road, load up everything I own, and drive off without anyone knowing about it until spring. That's also why I built such a strong fence."

Eddy noticed the frightened look on his friends' faces again. He liked that. If he really had to tell the truth, the idea of someone coming over that fence in the dark of night scared him just as much.

I sure hope that doesn't happen, he thought.

Chapter 3

Once the fires were going, everyone spent the next few hours settling in. The boys arranged sleeping bags in their room along with the warm ski suits, hats, gloves, and boots they'd brought along. It was pretty clear that, without the right clothes, a person could freeze to death after only a few minutes out in that cold.

The dads worked together to cook supper. In the fireplace a large iron pot, suspended over the fire from a hook, bubbled to the top with beef stew. Eddy's father baked cornbread in the kitchen stove.

"Where did you learn to cook like this?" Chet's father asked.

"In the army. I used to cook for a hundred and fifty men, three times a day. So doing the same thing for six people is nothing."

"Well, it sure smells good," Rusty said. "When do we eat?"

"About ten more minutes."

Soon they all formed a line near the fireplace. As they passed, Eddy's father scooped a steaming helping of stew onto their plates.

"Good thing you brought disposable plates," Rusty's dad complimented. "Washing the dishes up here would *not* be fun."

After dinner Chet asked, "What's that roar outside?"

"It's just the wind whipping through the trees, that's all. In the summer the leaves keep the gusts down some, but now there's nothing holding it back."

"Sounds kinda scary to me," Rusty said. "Like a bunch of hungry wolves or something."

"Well, why do you think they call this place Wolf Lake?"

"Really?"

"I wouldn't worry about it. Anyway, it's time for you boys to get to bed. We're going to try some ice fishing in the morning."

"But it's so cold," Rusty complained.

"That's okay. I have a little surprise for all of you," Eddy's father told them.

"A surprise. What surprise?"

"Now Rusty, if I told you, then it wouldn't be a surprise. Would it?"

The boys headed to their room for the night. Rusty and Chet had all kinds of questions.

"Have you come up here in the winter before?" Rusty asked.

"A few times," Eddy answered, "but it wasn't this cold before. I'll bet that ice out on the lake is at least ten feet thick."

"You said there would be lots of stuff to do," Rusty reminded him. "I'm still waiting for the list."

"My dad likes to tie a toboggan to the back of his car and pull kids on it."

"Think we could do that?" Chet asked.

"I don't see why not. There's more new snow up here than I've ever seen before. We might want to build a big fort. It's fun to hike across the lake on the ice, too. Some guys even drive their cars out there."

"Isn't that dangerous?" Rusty asked.

"You have to be careful, that's for sure. Wolf Lake has springs in some places. The water coming in from them is warmer and sometimes the ice isn't as thick there as in other places. I remember one time when a car was doing doughnuts on the ice one minute, and all of a sudden it went crashing right down through the ice."

"Then what happened?" Chet asked.

"Easy. It went to the bottom like a sack of rocks."

"How did they get it out?"

"Had to wait till warmer weather."

"You mean the car had to stay down there all winter?"

"Yup."

Rusty shuddered. "Man, I wouldn't want to fall through the ice. A guy could die."

"It happens up here sometimes."

"It does?"

"Sure. Usually to people on snowmobiles. That water is so cold, if you don't get to a warm place right away it'd be all over."

"This ice fishing doesn't sound like such a good idea to me," Rusty said.

"Aw, it'll be nothing. You'll see."

Though the wind continued howling even louder than before, the boys managed to fall asleep. That is until they heard a thump on the wall right outside their room.

"What was that?" Rusty whispered. Chet and Eddy were already sitting straight up, their eyes wide open.

Chet trembled. "There it goes again. Somebody should go look out the window."

"Why don't you do it?" Eddy asked.

Without warning, their door slowly creaked open. There weren't any lights on in the living room, and yet they could still see the shape of a man standing in the middle of the doorway. Instantly, all three boys dove beneath the safety of their sleeping bags.

"You boys all right?" a voice asked.

Eddy peered out as the light came on. "Dad?"

"I thought you might have heard the noise outside. I didn't want you to be scared."

"Who's scared?" Chet asked as he fumbled to get the sleeping bag off his head.

"Yeah, what's the big deal?" Rusty added in a muffled voice, but he was having trouble climbing out of his bag . . . backwards.

Eddy's father started to laugh. "It's just a deer. With all the snow this year they come in closer looking for food. He'll be gone soon."

Before long the boys went back to sleep. By morning the sun shone in through the windows in their room. No matter how hard they tried, Eddy and his friends couldn't stay asleep any longer. They smelled breakfast, too.

As they stumbled into the kitchen, their fathers were already sitting at the table drinking coffee.

"Breakfast in about five," Eddy's father announced. He had whipped up a batch of corn pancakes . . . not corn flavored. Eddy showed his friends that these had real corn in them. He'd also fixed some Canadian bacon and a batch of blueberry muffins.

"Shoot," Rusty said, "I could stay up here forever."

"Yeah, me too," Eddy added. "No more school."

"I wonder if Dillenger ever came up here?" Chet asked.

His father looked up. "Why would you ask that?"

"Oh, no reason really. It's just that we studied about him in history. There were some questions about his gang on our last test. With this place being out in the middle of nowhere, I just thought it would make a great hideout."

"You're giving me the creeps," Rusty complained. "Let's talk about something else."

Eddy's father interrupted, "After we eat, you boys need to get your warmest things on. We'll load our fishing gear onto the toboggan and drag it out onto the lake."

"But you said there was a surprise," Rusty reminded him.

"There will be. You'll see."

Breakfast was over and the boys began preparing for their wintry adventure. After pulling on their long underwear, double pants and socks, ski suits, hats, gloves, and heavy boots, the boys could hardly walk.

"I feel like an astronaut," Rusty complained.

"You'll be glad you have all that stuff on once we get outside," his father reminded him. Before long the fishermen were making fresh tracks in the snow.

"We look like the first Arctic explorers," Eddy announced proudly.

"At least we have a warm cabin to come back to," Rusty added.

On and on they trudged until the path opened onto Wolf Lake.

"We are going to freeze . . . to . . . death out here," Rusty complained. The wind blew in from the lake even harder than back at the cabin. Out here there was nothing to hold it back. Eddy and his friends looked out where sailboats skimmed across the ice as fast as cars.

"What are those?" Chet asked.

"Ice boats," his father told him.

As they stepped out of the heavy snow and onto the ice, it was easier to pull the toboggan. Now their load of supplies and equipment glided along smoothly.

"So, I'm ready f...f...f...for my surprise now," Rusty begged. Then he slipped and fell on the ice. Chet helped him get back up.

"Not much farther," Eddy's father announced.

After walking five more minutes, he stopped.

"There it is."

"There what is?" Rusty asked.

Eddy's father pointed, "Our ice shanty." Just ahead

sat about a dozen little huts out on the ice. They looked like a small village.

"We get to use one of those, Dad?" Eddy asked.

"I rented it for the days we're up here."

"Which is ours?"

"Should have number 56 on the door."

The boys stumbled ahead in their heavy suits until they found it. "Over here! It's over here!" After his father unlocked the door, Eddy pulled it open. Now it made sense why they had dragged so much firewood along. Over in the corner sat a wood-burning stove. The wood floor only went half-way across the hut. The rest was open to the frozen lake. Around the sides of the opening Eddy and the others saw wooden benches.

"I still don't understand why you brought your chainsaw, Dad," Chet commented.

"Eddy's dad asked me to bring it. You'll see why in a minute."

"First order of business is to start a fire. You boys may not believe it, but you won't be able to wear much more than your jeans and a T-shirt in here, once I get the fire going." As cold as it was outside, that idea didn't seem possible. Yet, soon after the fire began crackling, the boys had to start removing their heavy things. That was when Eddy's father brought in the chain saw.

"Leave the door open for a minute," he instructed. "We don't want to croak from the fumes."

No sooner had he said that than he gave a couple pulls on the start cord. The saw sputtered a couple of times, then roared to life. Eddy and his friends had to cover their ears.

Eddy's father lowered the blade toward the ice section of the floor. He gave the saw full power sending small pieces of ice flying in all directions. It didn't take long until he began cutting out small sections of ice. The other dads used hooks and clamps to grab those and throw them out the door.

The sun continued shining brightly outside their shanty. The sunlight gave a soft glow to everything under the ice. After Eddy's father skimmed the last slushy pieces of ice out of the hole, the boys stared down into the wonderland below.

"This is like a great big aquarium!" Rusty exclaimed.

"Yeah," Chet added, "except this is an aquarium you stand on top of, not next to."

The water was clear making it easy to see all the way to the bottom. "It reminds me of the glass bottom boat we went on in Florida that one time, Dad," Chet said.

"Only it was just a little warmer there," he chuckled.

"You boys need to be careful and look where you're

going. It's easy to forget yourself and step right off into the hole," Chet's dad cautioned.

"So how do we go fishing?" Rusty asked.

"Some people use spears. We're going to try fishing line and lures without the poles."

"We'd die if we fell in the water. How come the fish don't?"

"Fish are very adaptable. They slow down a lot in the cold, and they don't eat as much. In fact, most of them don't even grow all winter."

Each person found a place to sit and waited to see if anything might come swimming under the shack. After about an hour of this, the boys became restless.

"Is this all there is to it, Dad?" Eddy asked.

"Pretty much."

"Could we have something to eat then?"

"Sure. We packed sandwiches and other things in that box over there in the corner." That kept Eddy and his friends happy for a little longer. Then they tried fishing again. Rusty caught three small fish, but his dad made him throw them back. Then Chet's dad caught a whopper.

"What are we gonna do with the ones we catch?" Chet asked.

"Eat them, of course."

Around four in the afternoon the boys had had about

all the fishing *excitement* they could stand.

"Dad," Eddy began, "is it okay if we take the toboggan out on the lake for awhile?"

"Yes, but don't forget the ice isn't this thick everywhere. Be very careful."

"We will."

The boys quickly dressed again in their bulky clothes, strapped on their boots, and headed outside.

"Be back at the cabin by five," Eddy's father called out. As they walked outside, a cold gust of wind slammed the door shut.

The boys took turns giving toboggan rides. Two pulled while one skimmed across the ice. When they came to one area, the ice made a loud cracking noise.

"I don't like that sound at all," Rusty complained. "Let's get off this ice."

"You worry too much," Eddy teased. "Besides, it's my turn to ride. You're just trying to get out of pulling me."

"Whatever you say, Eddy. Hop on."

Eddy climbed onto the toboggan as his friends began pulling him like a couple of Alaskan sled dogs. Then suddenly, something terrible happened. As they were swinging the toboggan around in a big circle, the rope broke loose from one side sending Eddy flying off in the direction where they had first heard the ice crack.

"Eddy! Roll off!" Rusty pleaded.

But his friend decided to stay on and enjoy the ride. Then, the sound of a crack, much louder than before, thundered across the ice. Seconds after that, a hole opened up directly in front of Eddy. He rolled off the toboggan this time, but it was too late. The sled continued sailing across the ice, but Eddy didn't. The weight of his body and all those heavy clothes sent him crashing through the ice and into the icy waters.

Eddy had never felt such cold before. Like daggers in his chest, the frigid water made it almost impossible for him to breathe. His arms and legs were nearly useless until his brain switched into autopilot.

"Help me you guys!" Eddy screamed.

Chet hurried around the weakened area. He dashed to the toboggan, grabbed it, and then lay flat on the ice. From there he began to slither toward his friend, pulling the toboggan behind him.

"Hurry!" Rusty pleaded.

When he was close enough, Chet pulled the toboggan around in front if him, held on to the rope, and pushed the sled toward his friend.

"Grab it and hold on!" Rusty ordered.

Now Chet and Rusty tugged on the rope as hard as they could. Slowly Eddy was able to drag himself back up onto the ice.

"Now get on it," Chet called. He and Rusty first crawled, then stood to their feet. Chet quickly retied the other side of the rope. Then the boys began running back in the direction of the ice shanty. They screamed as loud as they could as they pulled Eddy across the ice.

"Help! Somebody help us!"

Chapter 4

Eddy was already shivering badly as his body struggled to keep warm. When they finally reached the shanty, their cries for help brought their fathers outside. They quickly helped Eddy into the hut where they removed his heavy, wet clothes. His entire body shook and had already begun to turn blue. Eddy's dad began to massage his arms and legs to get his blood circulating again.

"Quick! Get him something hot to drink!" Then he wrapped his son in a warm, dry blanket and placed him right next to the stove. It seemed like forever, but Eddy finally stopped shaking.

"You boys did a smart thing, bringing him here. If you'd tried to make it to the cabin . . . I don't know . . . I just don't know."

"I thought we told you to be careful," Rusty's father demanded.

"We were. It's just that one side of the rope came

loose. When it pulled out of our hands, he got away from us. That's when he hit the thin ice." Chet and Rusty were about to burst into tears.

"You guys lucked out," Eddy's father told them. "Next time you might not be so lucky."

The dads had caught enough fish for the day so they wrapped Eddy up in a couple more blankets and loaded him on the toboggan. His wet, frozen clothes were stacked on the back where they sat straight up all by themselves. His father locked the shanty door. Everyone headed back toward the cabin. It was starting to get dark when they finally reached the front door. Eddy was quickly carried inside as the others followed.

Typical of a boy his age, and even though he could have drowned, Eddy already wanted to know, "What's for dinner?"

"We're having a cookout," his father told him.

"It's too cold to cook out," Rusty said.

"You'll see."

Eddy's father cut several small branches from a tree near the front porch and brought them inside. With his sharp knife he whittled the ends until they were as sharp as spears. The other fathers were busy slicing open hotdog buns, spreading out plates, and all the usual things needed for a good cookout.

"Hey," Eddy said. "This isn't a cookout. Looks more like a *cook in* to me."

"You're exactly right," his father told him.

For the next hour they roasted hotdogs over a blazing fire in the fireplace. After dinner, the boys toasted marshmallows and ate them until there was no more room in any of their stomachs . . . not even for the smallest belch.

"I gotta go lie down," Rusty groaned as he and the other boys slumped to the floor. No one moved for the longest time while they waited for the mountain of food they'd eaten to settle.

Later, Eddy had an idea. "You guys wanna play a game or something?"

"Sure," Chet answered. "Whadaya have up here?"

"I brought a new game I just got for Christmas."

"What is it?" Rusty asked.

"It's called Pokey."

Rusty wrinkled up his nose. "Pokey? What kind of a name is that?"

"It's pretty cool, really."

"So how do you play it?" Chet asked.

Eddy went into the other room and brought back a box. He took off the top and pulled out a board, some game pieces, and two stacks of cards. "This game isn't like anything you've played before," he began. "You guys remember playing checkers?"

"Checkers," Rusty sneered. " *Oh, please!* Who plays checkers?"

"Fine, but you know how that game is played, right?"

"Of course."

"Ever play giveaway?"

"What does that have to do with Pokey?" Chet asked.

"Well, you play most games to see who can finish the fastest. In Pokey the winner is the one who can finish last."

"Oh, I see," Rusty said. "So you move as slow as you can."

"Now you've got it," Eddy said.

He opened the game board and placed a stack of red and a stack of green cards in their places. "The red cards slow you down, and the green cards make you go faster."

The game board had paths that could take a player off in all kinds of directions. Eddy showed his friends the rest area, mountain trail, a campsite, jail, and other places to slow down a player. But there were also shortcuts and ladders where they would have to move ahead faster.

"This looks kinda fun," Chet said.

Next, Eddy placed the game pieces in the center of the board. "You can be a turtle, a jar of molasses, a snail, an old car, a crawling baby, or this hot-air balloon."

"I'll take the snail," Rusty said.

Chet looked for a moment. "Give me the turtle."

Eddy chose the old car. Then he placed a spinner in the center of the board. "We use this to tell how many spaces to move, but we can also use it to decide who goes first."

The spinner had numbers from one to six. "Highest goes last. No, wait. Since we want to go slow, let's make it the lowest goes last."

"Lowest is the slowest," Rusty joked.

The boys spun the dial. Chet got a two, Rusty stopped on the five, and Eddy stopped on the six.

Chet smiled. "Looks like you go first, Eddy."

"What are you talking about? I said the highest number went last."

Rusty broke in. "But you changed it to . . ."

"I did not," Eddy fumed.

"You are such a cheater," Chet told him. "Let's play the dumb game anyway."

"Read the rules," Rusty said. "Their rules, not yours."

"It's like I said. You want to finish last. The green cards make you do faster things like take a short cut, take an extra turn, get on a bullet train, things like that."

"What are some of the slow things?" Rusty asked.

Eddy turned over a few of the red cards. "Pull a donkey over a bridge. Stop and take a picture. Explore a cave. Go backward three spaces."

"Okay. Let's get started," Chet said.

For the next hour and a half the boys played. With each turn they tried to move as slowly as possible. Several times both of his friends complained when they caught Eddy trying to cheat. Later, as he was about to finish first and lose the game, Eddy pretended to sneeze. When he did that, he also knocked the game off the table. Cards and game pieces scattered across the wood floor.

"You did that on purpose," Rusty complained.

"I did not! Must be because I fell through the ice."

"Eddy, you're the biggest cheater I ever saw," Rusty continued. "Once . . . just once . . . I'd like to see you do the right thing. You should try it sometime, just so you know how it feels." Then he stomped out of the room.

"Hey, Chet, you want to play again?" Eddy asked. "I can set it up like it was and we could finish our game."

His friend didn't show any interest and left the room. "Fine. Then I'll put it away." Eddy gathered up all the stray pieces and placed them, along with the board, back in the box. He went into the living room and sat by the fire with his friends.

Eddy's father was listening to a radio he had brought so they could keep up on the weather.

"Tonight," the announcer began, "we can expect

rising temperatures followed by snow that will begin falling before dawn. Expect heavy wet snow throughout the day followed by extremely cold temperatures on the back side of this system."

"So, Dad, what are we going to do tomorrow?" Eddy asked.

"I thought later in the morning we could hook the toboggan behind the truck, and I'll pull you boys around on some of the dirt roads in the area."

"Is that dangerous?" Rusty asked.

"Not really."

"But what about other cars?"

"Exactly how many of those have you seen up here so far?"

"Oh, right."

"Anyway, I've done this for years. We don't go too fast, and we pretty much have the whole area to ourselves. You'll be safe."

Eddy saw that while he and his friends were sitting by the fire, his father had set a few things out on the kitchen table. "Is this what I think it is?" Eddy asked.

"Snow ice cream!" his father called to the others. Then he brought in an enormous bowl filled with fresh snow.

"How do we make it?" Rusty asked.

As he demonstrated each step, Eddy's father

instructed, "You take some snow, mix in a little milk, sugar, vanilla, and sprinkles." Then he held the bowl into the air. "I give you . . . snow ice cream."

Everyone gathered around the warm fireplace to try the new dessert. Eddy's father asked the group, "Anyone got a campfire story about winter?"

"We don't have a campfire," Rusty said.

"Think of it as an indoor campfire . . . unless you'd like to move this party outside."

Rusty only shivered and moved closer to the fire.

"I have one," Chet's father said. "Did you boys know that out of all the millions and millions of snowflakes God made, no two are exactly alike?"

"Is that true?" Rusty asked.

"It's one more indication of the amazing creation God has made for us to enjoy."

Oh, brother, Eddy thought.

"I know a pretty scary winter story," Rusty's father said.

Eddy grinned. "That's more like it."

"I've been reading this book called *Tales of Terror*."

"I don't know, Dad."

"Quiet, Russ. There was a 26 year old man who loved mountain climbing. His infant son had recently been born, and the man's wife didn't want her husband to go on a climbing trip he had planned. 'Please stay home,' she begged."

"I would have gone," Eddy said.

"No matter how much she cried, the man went anyway. All was fine until, when he was climbing the face of a glacier, he slipped and fell into a hole in the ice."

"Did the rescuers get him out?" Chet asked.

"No, he died down there. Not only that, the place where he fell made it impossible for anyone to reach him. So, the rescuers decided to come back in the spring and try again, but when they returned, they couldn't find the body."

"What happened to him?" Rusty whispered.

"No one knew for sure. Years later, after the young son grew up, he became obsessed with finding the body of his long lost father. Year after year he traveled to the mountains, and each year he failed in his search. Then one spring, when the son was nearly 60 years old, he decided to make one final try."

"He should have given up," Rusty said.

"You'd come looking for me, wouldn't you Russ?" his father asked.

"Anyway, the old son needed friends to help him climb to the spot where his father had died. He finally made it. All out of breath he sat on the ice. As he reached down to tie one of his boots, he saw something."

"What?" Rusty asked in a whisper.

"At first he brushed a little snow off the ice. There was no mistake. Staring right back at him from inside the ice was the frozen face of a young man."

"Was it his father?" Chet asked.

"The son's friends worked the rest of the day to chop away the ice. When they finished, the son was now staring at a face that looked just like him when he was about that age. Then the son realized that he was sixty years old and looking into the face of his father which now looked 34 years younger than his own."

"How awful," Rusty whispered again. "Then what happened?"

Rusty's father hesitated for the longest time. All at once he shouted, "The son . . . went . . . maaad!"

The boys screamed and raced around the room.

"Calm down, boys." Chet's father said, "It's time for you to hit the sack. You've had a big day, especially Eddy."

Eddy and his friends continued chattering as they went to their room. They talked together after they'd climbed into their sleeping bags for the night.

"Your dad tells the scariest stories," Eddy said.

Rusty sighed. "I know."

"This is a fun place," Chet said. "I'm glad we came

up here."

"Yeah, except for Eddy trying to turn himself into a human ice cube," Rusty added.

"It's a good thing you guys got me out," Eddy said. "I don't know what I'd have done without you there to save me."

"I'm glad too," Chet told him.

It was quiet for a few minutes. Then Rusty said, "I was just thinking."

"About what?" Chet asked.

"About Eddy."

"What about me?"

"I was thinking, you're such a big cheater, you even figured out a way to cheat death this afternoon."

"That's not funny," Eddy grumbled.

"Well, you are."

"One thing's for sure," Chet said. "At least we know that's the worst thing that could happen to us up here."

"You're right about that," Rusty agreed.

Eddy thought for a moment, "I sure hope so."

Chet yawned and stretched. "Me, too. Now go to sleep. Will ya?"

Chapter 5

When the boys awakened the next morning, they looked outside to find the weather report was exactly right. Heavy wet snowflakes plopped to the ground like millions of paratroopers falling from the sky. A strong wind blew through the trees again causing a roar like never ending thunder.

"Can we still go tobogganing, Dad?" Eddy asked as he walked into the kitchen.

"Sure thing. We've got the four-wheel-drive. Remember?"

"Great. What's for breakfast?"

"I've made a mountain of scrambled eggs, a loaf of toast, and a bucket of juice."

"Did you like cooking for all those guys in the army?" Chet asked.

"Most of the time, but not always."

"Why not always?" Rusty asked.

"Because some of the food made a real mess. It was the cleanup I hated."

"But up here we throw all the paper junk in the fireplace," Eddy said.

"We had some guys who'd throw perfectly good pans away if they were too hard to clean."

"Really?" Rusty asked. "Isn't that kind of cheating?"

"Yeah, I guess it is. Come on, let's dig in."

The boys ate like this was the last food they might see all day . . . maybe even for the rest of their lives. After they finished and everything was cleared away, Eddy's father told them, "Time to get your warm stuff on again."

"Great!" Rusty shouted as he and the others raced for their room.

"Double pants, double socks, heavy snowsuits, gloves, and boots," he reminded them.

It took a long time to do it, but when the boys finally had everything on, they struggled just to walk out of their room.

"We look like those guys in Sumo wrestler suits," Chet joked. They started running into each other, bounced off, hit the floor, and then did it over and over again.

All out of breath, Rusty demanded, "Let's hurry up."

"Are you that excited about tobogganing?" Eddy asked.

"No! I'm burning up in all these clothes."

The boys waddled toward the front door like three plump penguins. Outside, Eddy's father had tied the toboggan to the back bumper. Chet's and Rusty's fathers were already sitting in the truck where it was warm.

Even though the snow was wet, it made a crunch, crunch, crunching sound under the boy's heavy boots as they trudged toward the truck.

"Hop on and we'll get started," Eddy's father told them. Eddy and his friends found their places on the toboggan as his father climbed into his truck and slammed the door. Eddy looked up to see Rusty's father sitting in the middle seat where he could be the spotter in case anyone fell off.

"Your dad plans to go real slow?" Rusty asked quivering. "Right?"

"No problem," Eddy answered.

The truck did pull them slowly at first. The boys found ropes on each side where they held on. Since they were only sitting on thin boards that were whizzing along the hard, frozen ground, it was a rough ride, especially whenever they hit a big bump.

Then Eddy called out, "Faster! Faster!" His father pushed his foot on the gas, and they went streaking off at what felt like a hundred miles an hour.

"We're really flying now," Chet called out. "Good thing this is a straight road."

No sooner had he finished saying that than all three boys noticed the road was about to take a sharp turn.

"Hold on!" Rusty yelled. As the car rounded the curve, their toboggan swung out making an even wider turn. The boys went off the road and jumped a snow ridge. Their toboggan flew high into the air, then slammed back to the ground. Its nose dove under a big drift, spraying snow high into the air.

The boys howled with laughter until they all noticed it at the same time.

"Trees! Dead ahead!" Eddy warned.

"Bail out!" Rusty screamed.

They rolled off the sled like one big log just seconds before the toboggan glanced off a tree so hard it went flying into the air like a glider. Then it struck another tree sending the toboggan careening back onto the road. By that time the truck had come to a stop. The toboggan simply glided right under the back bumper and came to a stop.

"That was a close one," Eddy's father called out as he ran to them. "Everyone all right?"

Rusty stood up first and started brushing snow off of everywhere. "We think so."

"Want to quit?"

"Are you kidding? This is great," Chet said as he struggled to get back on his feet. With the help of their fathers the boys pulled out the snow that had crammed into their hoods, boots, and sleeves. Soon they were back on the toboggan and ready to go. Again the truck pulled forward and away they streaked. As they rounded another turn, the toboggan hit a bump. This time the boys hung on. As they slammed back to the ground, Chet lost his hold on the ropes and fell off.

"Man overboard! Man overboard!" Eddy yelled, and the truck came to a stop so Chet could catch up and get back on again.

After riding together for a long time Eddy asked, "You guys want to ride one at a time?"

"Sure," Rusty said.

"Me first," Eddy demanded.

Rusty groaned. "That figures."

It was a little easier to steer the toboggan with just one guy on it. Eddy lay flat on his stomach with his arms out front as he looked over the nose of the toboggan. When the truck turned, he tugged on one side of the rope. That made the toboggan turn slightly in the direction of the rope he was pulling. Eddy not only cheated death when he fell through the ice, he liked to take chances, too. Slowly he steered the toboggan right up to the tall snow ridge on one side of the road. Then with a quick jerk on the rope he jumped the toboggan up on top of the ridge.

Now he looked more like a surfer in Hawaii than a guy with snow flying in all directions. When he tried to pull back off the ridge, the toboggan dipped too low to one side and flipped over sending Eddy sprawling across the road. He slammed into the other ridge and came to a stop. When his friends reached him, he was still laughing.

"You're really something, you know that?" Chet said.

"Who's next?" Eddy asked.

The other boys took fewer chances, but they still had fun. Finally, it was time to head back to the cabin for lunch. "That was a lot of fun, Mr. Thompson. Thanks. I had a great time." Chet said.

"So *did* I," Rusty added.

When they returned to the cabin, the boys went in their room to remove all their heavy clothes and get ready to eat lunch. Eddy's father came to their door. "What do you boys want to do this afternoon?"

"I have an idea," Eddy told him. "Why?"

"Well, we plan to do some more fishing. You want to come with us?"

"No thanks, Dad. We have other plans."

"Fine with me." He went back to the kitchen.

"Other plans?" Chet asked.

"Yeah, what other plans?" Rusty added.

"First, I thought we could build a snow man in the front yard. That snow is so wet. It's great for packing."

"I'm up for that," Chet told him.

After lunch the dads headed back toward the lake while the boys got ready to go back out in the snow. They didn't wear as many heavy clothes as before because now they could duck into the cabin to warm up if they needed to.

"We should stay pretty warm if we're moving around and working," Eddy suggested. He and his friends found out that was true as they began rolling the snow into three heavy balls.

Chet grunted as they lifted the middle ball on top of the bottom one. "I wondered how those people I've seen skiing in the mountains could run around with just a sweater on, but I'm getting hot in this snowmobile suit.

"Let's take a break after we get the three sections together," Eddy suggested.

A few minutes later they went inside, not to warm up, but to cool off. The boys were thirsty, too. They sat around the kitchen table drinking juice.

"I'm really glad our dads are here with us," Chet began.

"Yeah," Rusty sighed, "this place is kinda scary."

"What do you mean?" Eddy asked.

"Well, there aren't any other people up here."

"So?"

"So, if somebody bad came along there wouldn't be anyone around to help us."

"Help us what?"

"I don't know. It's just that I'd be afraid, that's all."

"We don't have to be afraid, no matter what happens," Chet told them.

"Here we go," Eddy sneered.

"What do you mean, 'here we go?'" Rusty asked.

"Oh, he's going to tell us God can take care of us. Well, I'll tell you what I think. I think I can take care of myself. Anyway I have to."

"Even if what you do isn't right?" Rusty asked.

"You spend an awful lot of time worrying about me, don't you, Russ."

"Anybody who cheats like you do couldn't expect God to help him out, even if you get in big trouble."

"What are you talking about?"

"Tell him, Chet."

"You know that Rusty and I go to the same church?"

"Big deal."

"It's just that our last Sunday school lesson was about honor."

"What about it?"

"Our teacher told us how important it is to have a good name."

Eddy laughed. "You probably mean like Joseph, or David."

"No. It isn't the name itself that matters. It's the person who has the name."

"I don't get it," Eddy grumbled.

"We learned that a person gets a good name or a bad one by how they act and what they do."

"So what?"

Rusty broke in, "It's like the way you cheat at everything. I mean, that's what kids at school think when they hear your name . . . Eddy the cheater."

"You want me to smack you one?"

"No, I'm just trying to show you what a bad name can do."

"If you're saying I have a bad name. . . ."

"Listen," Chet interrupted. "It isn't like you can't change it. It's just that you'll have a harder time than if you didn't try to cheat at everything in the first place."

"Don't you start, too," Eddy warned. "Besides, I've listened to about all I can stand for one trip. Let's go back outside. I have an idea for something you're not going to believe."

Chapter 6

The boys pulled on their snowsuits again and went back outside. They worked hard to finish making their snowman in the front yard.

As they finished, Rusty finally grumbled, "I thought you said you had a great idea."

Eddy turned and silently walked around back while the others followed him to the small porch where firewood was neatly stacked. From one corner he pulled out three wooden crates and two shovels.

"What are we doing now?" Rusty asked.

"I'll show you. Come with me."

Eddy led his friends all the way to the back part of the yard and to the fence that ran along the abandoned narrow road behind the cabin.

"Rusty," Eddy teased, "you'd get good and scared if this fence wasn't here. There'd be nothing to keep out the monsters, wolves, and robbers you're so worried about."

"Funny, Edward. Real funny," Rusty scoffed. "So, what are we doing back here?"

"You see how the snow is drifted up against the fence?"

"That's like asking me if I think it's cold out here. Yes, I see the drift."

"Then what we're gonna do is dig out the drift first."

"What are the crates for?" Chet asked. "To sit on?"

"Plenty of time for you to know about that. Start digging."

The boys took turns digging deep into the drift until they came right up to the fence. "This will be the back wall of our new snow fort," Eddy announced.

"Snow fort?" Rusty said. "That sounds great."

Eddy laughed. "Finally, something Russell actually likes."

"Keep digging," Rusty told them.

They cleared enough snow to form a big square. Then Eddy picked up the crates and gave one to each of his friends. "Since the new snow is so wet and heavy, we can pack it in these crates."

"Oh, I get it," Chet said.

"You wanna help me to get it?" Rusty complained.

Eddy just stared at his friend at first. "We fill our crates with snow, pack it down real hard, and. . . ."

"Now I see," Rusty broke in. "We make . . . kind of like building blocks."

"Not kind of like . . . they *are* blocks. Then we can build the walls as high as we want."

"I like it," Rusty said.

Eddy opened his mouth to say something sarcastic, but Rusty cut in, "Keep it to yourself."

Their work started out slowly as they tried different ways of stacking the snow blocks, but soon the boys worked like a professional construction crew. One boy shoveled snow and packed it into the crates as the other two hauled them to the fort. The more they worked, the higher the walls went. After a couple of hours the boys decided to take a break. They sat on their crates near the snow walls.

"How high should we build it?" Chet asked.

"High enough so we can stand up inside," Eddy answered.

"No fair," Rusty complained. "You guys are at least a foot taller than me."

"My dad told me he heard it's gonna get really cold again tonight. That means this wet snow we're stacking is going to freeze solid. Our fort will be like a real building."

"Cool," Rusty said.

"It's snow, Russ. Of course, it's cool," Eddy teased.

"You guys go ahead and keep building. I'm going to

pull in some of the long dead tree branches we use for firewood. We can lay those across the top, cover them with snow, and no one will know we even *have* a fort back here."

Rusty started to say, "Coo . . . Never mind," he chuckled.

The roof went on faster than Eddy thought it would. The boys covered it with loose snow. "Now all we gotta do is build the front wall, make a door, and we're in," Eddy announced with pride.

"Eddy!" a voice called. "Where are you guys?"

"Back here, Dad."

Eddy's father came around into the yard. "Wow! I see you boys have been busy."

"How was the fishing?"

"We caught enough to make dinner. Us dads are going to run into town to pick up a few things at the store. You boys want to ride along?"

"No, thanks. We'd like to finish the front before it gets cold tonight."

"Suit yourselves. We'll be back after dark, but I plan to cook a full fish dinner so don't snack on anything."

"We won't even have time to go in the cabin, Dad."

"All right. See you architects later."

A few minutes later the boys heard the doors to the truck slam shut. Then it drove away.

"Glad we stayed," Chet said. "This is a lot more fun."

They continued building even as the sun went down. The air began getting much colder, but with the air came a clear night sky. The moon, shining against the snow, gave them all the light they needed to keep right on building. Since their fathers went into town while it was still daytime, they hadn't left any of the lights on. The inside of the cabin was completely dark, making the place look like it was abandoned.

Just as they finished the doorway, an unexpected sound caused the boys to turn around and look in the same direction at the same time. Someone was coming but not on the road out in front of the cabin. A truck drove up just on the other side of the fence.

"They couldn't be back this soon, could they?" Rusty asked.

"No," Eddy answered. "They wouldn't be driving back there either. My dad never does that."

"Maybe he's just trying to scare us," Chet suggested.

"Well, they're doing a pretty good job of it," Rusty groaned.

Eddy held his finger up to his lips. "Shhh," he warned.

The lights on the truck went off, but its engine kept running.

"Who do you think it is?" Chet whispered.

"Cops?" Rusty suggested.

"Not likely," Eddy answered. "My dad said they don't come out here in the winter." He motioned for the boys to follow him into the fort. They inched their way in the dark until they were right up against the fence. Then they each found a crack between the boards where they could peer through to the other side. The boys looked out just in time to see two dark figures still sitting in the front seat of a double cab pickup truck, waving their arms around.

"Looks like they're arguing," Chet said. "What should we do?"

"We just sit tight," Eddy whispered.

Then the driver put the truck in reverse and backed up a few feet. He shifted into another gear and turned the front wheels toward the fence. The tires bit deep into the snow as the truck lunged forward.

"He's going to crash into the fence and crush us," Rusty squeaked. But the wheels turned away from the fence as the truck pulled in right next to it. The man on the passenger side opened his door and stepped out into the snow. His feet made a crunching sound as he came around the back of the truck. Then he climbed up into the bed of the truck and stood looking over the fence.

The driver opened his window. "What can you see?"

"Nothin', Boss."

"What do you mean . . . nothing?"

"I mean I can't see nothin'."

"Lean up against the fence and look over. See what's on the other side."

The air was already cold, and the snow fort was no tropical beach either. But when the man said, "See what's on the other side," Eddy felt like the temperature went down another twenty degrees. He figured his friends thought the same thing because all three of them got a bad case of the shivers at the very same time.

They pressed against the fence tightly so they could look up at the man. Just then the man standing on the truck bumped against the boards. It was like a donkey had kicked the fence. The boys fell onto their backs as chunks of snow fell down through the roof. They quickly scrambled back up to see what would happen next.

That's when Eddy noticed he could see his breath in the frigid night air. He figured if he could see it, the two men might see it, too, as it went out through the crack in the fence. Eddy reached out and touched his friends on their shoulders. But when he did, it scared them so bad they fell backward into the snow a second time.

"Breathe down the front of your jackets," he whispered. When they did that, the steam went away.

"Der ain't nothin' over der, Boss," the man said.

"Everybody knows these cabins are only for summer people," the man in the truck answered. "A person could die out here, and no one would know about it till spring."

"Whadaya want me ta do, Boss?"

"Come on back down while I think of a plan." He slammed the truck into park, but when he did that, it lurched forward just enough so that the man standing in the back lost his balance. The boys watched as he went flying head-first off the back of the truck, landing in a deep drift. Only his feet stuck out.

The boys started laughing so hard they knew they were sure to be discovered. It was a good thing they decided to start breathing into their jackets because that helped muffle some of the sound. Of course, the poor sap in the snowdrift couldn't hear a thing. He was buried so deeply, the boys could hardly hear his cries for help as he struggled in the snow.

Eddy stopped laughing, but his chest hurt from trying to keep it in. Tears streamed down his face threatening to turn him into an ice sculpture.

The driver moved his truck away from the fence. When he stepped out and walked back to help his human snowplow partner, Eddy noticed that he was taller than the other man. The man in the snow was not too small . . . not around anyway. He was just much shorter and heavier.

When he finally got out of the snow, it was clear to see he was angry because he never stopped yelling.

"Ya did dat on purpose. Dat's da meanest trick ya never done."

"Ever done. It's ever done, Clarence."

"I don't care. I ain't never gonna forget it."

"Will *you* keep your *voice* down!"

"What for? Ya tink the squirrels is gonna rat on us?"

"You never know who might be back here. We can't leave no witnesses."

That really scared Eddy. Now he knew these guys weren't just joking around.

"Look, Clarence, I'll buy you a hamburger when we get out of here. Will that make it better?"

"Gee, tanks, Boss."

Faintly, in the distance, Eddy thought he heard something. He pointed in the direction of the sound, then shrugged his shoulders. What he heard sounded like hundreds of police sirens, and they were coming his way.

"Aw, Boss. Now whadaya gonna do, huh?"

"Be quiet and let me think," he thundered. Then he snapped his fingers. "I got it."

"Whadaya got, Boss?"

"Get me the briefcase! Hurry!"

"My . . . my name's Clarence, not Hurry."

"Just do it!"

The fat short man bounded to the other side of the truck, slipped and fell, got up again, opened the back door, and returned with a shiny metal case.

"But dis is all we got," he complained.

"Yeah, but if the cops catch us with it, we'll have nothing. Now give it to me."

"I don't know, Boss."

"There's a hamburger in it for you. Remember?"

"Dat's right. I almost forgot to forget. I mean remember. I mean. . . ."

"Just hand it over."

With each passing second the sirens kept coming closer. The larger man took the case and held it in both hands. "The way I figure it, there ain't nobody here. And there ain't *gonna* be nobody around for months. This case will be safer out here than in the truck."

"How ya know dat?

"At least, if we leave it here, we know where it is."

"Yeah, it's not wit us."

"Right. But it ain't in the truck neither."

"Tell me why dats s'posed ta make me happy?"

"Because if the cops catch up with us, they ain't gonna find nothin' on us. That's why."

"I still ain't happy, Boss."

The police were close enough now that the boys could faintly see their lights flashing against the snow through the trees.

"We ain't got no choice, and we ain't got no time, Clarence. Now, take this thing and throw it as hard as you can over the fence."

Over the fence, Eddy thought. *That can't be good.*

Now the police were on the same narrow lane heading straight toward the crooks' truck.

"Throw it, Clarence! Throw it!"

The boys watched as the short fat man swung the case high over his head. He spun around and around as the moonlight shone against the bright metal finish on the case. With one giant heave and a loud grunt, he let it go sailing over the fence. But all that spinning around must have made him dizzy because he plopped right down in the snow.

As he hit the ground, there was another loud thump directly on top of the roof the boys had built over their fort.

I'm glad we got that part finished, Eddy thought.

The fat man tried to jump to his feet, but he fell right back down again. It reminded Eddy of how he and his friends spun round and round at school to see how dizzy they could get. Then they'd try to race across a line to see who finished first. Rusty was always last.

The man stood up again, and again he plopped right

back down.

"Clarence, we gotta go. Hurry!"

"I'm hurryin'. I'm hurryin'."

"You've been in the same spot forever. Move it!"

Clarence stood once again and this time he was able to move forward. But he slammed right into the side of the truck so hard he put a big dent in the door. That made him bounce right off, and he was back in the snow again.

"Hamburger, Clarence. Hamburger!"

Clarence got back to his feet somehow, stumbled around to the other door and fell in as the truck roared away with just a second to spare. Clarence was still hanging half in and half out of his door.

The boys watched in wonder as enough light to power a small town raced past their hideout. The sirens let out a head-splitting shriek that was so loud they had to cover their ears. As quickly as the police had come, they now faded into the distance. Then the boys heard footsteps crunching in the snow outside their fort. From the sound of it, Eddy thought at least three people were coming.

"Hide in the corner," he warned.

The boys huddled together as they shivered like wet dogs. Then a voice called, "Anybody in there?"

"Dad?" Eddy asked nervously.

"Yes. We just got home. What in the world just

happened back here?"

Eddy whispered to his friends, "Don't say anything about the case yet."

"It was really something, Dad," he called out.

The boys crawled toward the entrance and out the door.

"This is quite a fortress you've built," Rusty's father said. "It has a roof and everything."

The boys looked up to see if the silver case was still up there. It was, but the way it fell on the roof, the case was almost completely covered with snow. Eddy figured if he could hardly see it and he knew it was up there, then his dad wasn't likely to spot it.

"Come on. Let's go inside the cabin. It's really cold out here. Then you boys can tell us all about it."

They turned and headed back toward the cabin. All except Eddy who quickly climbed up one side of the fort, grabbed the heavy case, slid back down, and tossed it through the front entrance. Then he hurried to catch up with the others.

"What do you think is inside?" Rusty whispered.

"Yes, let's get inside," Eddy's father answered.

Eddy shrugged his shoulders. "Whatever it is, now it belongs to us."

"What did you say?" his father asked.

"I . . . I'm sure glad this cabin belongs to us."

Chapter 7

Eddy's father out-did himself with dinner, cooking the fish in a thick, cornmeal batter. He made rice and vegetables. He even baked a cherry crisp with juicy, red cherries, oatmeal, brown sugar, butter, and walnuts. But even with all the delicious food, the boys found it nearly impossible to think about anything besides that case setting out there in the snow, all by itself. They hardly ate anything.

What if somebody climbs over the fence and steals it, Eddy wondered.

"I thought you boys would be famished," Eddy's father said with a disappointed tone in his voice.

"It isn't the food, Dad. Food's great."

"Then what?"

"Must have been all the excitement with the police and everything," Eddy answered.

"Yeah," Rusty added. "Those two bums came right up to your fence with their truck."

"They did? What for?"

"I think they might have stolen something."

"I see. Well, the police will have no trouble tracking them in all this snow. Probably caught the guys already."

"Man, I sure hope so," Rusty sighed.

"We plan to go out fishing again tomorrow," Chet's father told them. "How about you guys? Got any big plans?"

"We thought we could stay here and work on the fort some more," Eddy said.

"That's fine with us, but no more exciting police chases. Okay? We've had enough of those for one trip."

"For our whole lives," Rusty added.

They began clearing away the table. Eddy went around and scooped up all the paper plates. Then he walked over to the fireplace. "I love doing the dishes up here," he said as he threw his stack of plates into the fire.

The boys went to their room early. Not because they were so tired. They needed to talk. Later, even though they tried to sleep, no one could.

"What do you think we should do about the case," Chet asked.

Eddy answered first. "I think we need to see what's inside. We can decide from there."

"Why do we need to see what's inside before we decide?"

"We just have to! Okay? Now go to sleep."

But the boys continued whispering late into the night. The slightest sound outside their cabin sent them rushing to the window to see who or what was out there. It turned out to be the wind every time.

After a sleepless night that seemed to last almost forever, the sun finally started coming up. Shadows from the window frames stretched across the floor.

"Let's eat as fast as we can and get outside," Eddy instructed. Instead, they decided to take their time at breakfast and at least wait until the fishing party left for the day. As soon as they were alone, the boys dashed to their room, threw on a few warm things, and burst out the back door.

"Are you sure it's still there?" Rusty asked.

"Unless those guys came back in the dark," Eddy called over his shoulder. He was the first one to dive through the entrance to their fort. Chet and Rusty nearly fell in on top of him.

"It's still here," Eddy reported. He grabbed the mysterious case and laid it across his legs as he sat on one of the crates.

"What do you think's inside?" Chet asked.

"I don't know but we're about to find out," Eddy said. He pushed in on both latches, but they didn't open. "Those creeps locked it."

"Maybe there's a bomb in there," Rusty shuddered.

"I doubt it."

"Well, how would *you* know?"

"Because. Do you think Stupid and Son of Stupid looked like they knew how to handle a bomb?"

"Sure," Chet added, "and they threw the thing over the fence. A bomb would have gone off . . . wouldn't it?"

"Good point," Rusty said.

Eddy thought for a second. "My dad has a few tools in the cellar of our cabin."

"You mean there's a downstairs? Man, that gives me a creepy feeling," Rusty said.

"Everything gives you a creepy feeling," Chet teased.

The boys rushed across the snow and back into the cabin. Eddy led them through the kitchen and into a storage room. He walked to the center of the room, leaned down, pulled a rug out of the way, and took hold of a black metal ring in the floor. When he pulled on it, a trap door opened.

"Follow me," he said as he disappeared down the ladder and into the dark.

Rusty suggested, "Maybe somebody should stay up here and keep watch."

"Get down here," Eddy called back.

"Come on," Chet encouraged. "It'll be okay."

"Close the door behind you," Eddy ordered.

"Are you crazy?" Rusty said in protest.

"Just do it. And pull on that string connected to the rug. It covers over the trap door."

As Eddy struck a match and lit an oil lamp, Rusty slowly pulled the door closed over his head. Eddy placed the lamp on a small workbench against a dirt wall. Then, he tried to slam the case against the hard floor to see if it would break open. Nothing happened, except for making dents in the side from hitting the floor.

"That's not gonna work," Chet said.

"You got any ideas, genius?"

"We need to break the locks somehow."

"Be my guest."

Chet grabbed the biggest hammer he could find. He looked around on the table and picked up a chisel. After placing the sharp blade of the chisel against the first lock, he took a big swing. The hammer only glanced off the top of the chisel striking him on his wrist.

"Ouch! Man that hurts!" He dropped the hammer and held on to his throbbing wrist.

"Let me try it. I can open anything," Rusty boasted. He didn't bother with anything but the hammer. With it he began smashing into the lock on one side. A few seconds later that one popped right open.

"You did it!" Chet yelled.

"Keep it down," Eddy cautioned.

Rusty stood proudly over the case. "One down. One lock to go." He hauled off and beat the tar out of the second lock until it, too, gave up without much of a fight.

"Let's get it back up on the bench," Eddy ordered. He lifted the case from the floor and placed it next to the lamp. The other boys moved in closer as all eyes were riveted on the silver, somewhat battered case.

Eddy reached out and placed both hands on the top. He was about to lift it when the boys heard footsteps on the floor directly above their heads.

"Think it's your dad?" Chet asked.

Eddy looked at his watch. "Can't be. They aren't coming back for hours."

"At least no one will know we're down here."

"Guys," Rusty whispered.

"Not now, Russ."

"But it's important."

The steps suddenly stopped.

"Eddy," Rusty persisted.

"If we just be quiet, no one will ever know where we are."

"I gotta tell you something," Rusty whispered again.

"What *is* it?" Eddy shot back.

Rusty swallowed real hard. "I . . . I forgot to pull on the string."

"You what?"

The next thing that happened was so terrifying all they could do was close their eyes. Eddy peaked out of just one eyelid as the trap door creaked, then began slowly opening.

"Who's down there?" a voice demanded. "You'd better come out right now!"

Eddy thought it sounded like his dad, but he wasn't sure. His friends looked too scared to think of anything besides being scared.

"Eddy, you down there?"

"Dad?"

"Yeah. What are you doing down there?"

"What happened to your voice?"

"That's why I came back. I need some cough drops. What are you doing, son?"

"The guys didn't know this place was here. I . . . I was just showing them around."

"You know I don't like you messing with my tools. Now come on up." Eddy took a second to slip the case under some old boxes. He and his friends scampered up the ladder. When they got to the top, they all tried to act like nothing was wrong. As soon as Eddy's father left to go back to the ice shanty, the boys raced back down the ladder.

"That was a close one, Eddy," Rusty said.

"I know. Now let's get this baby open," he said as he lit the lamp again. As before, they gathered around the case. Eddy reached out and prepared to open the top. Then he hesitated. "How we gonna split this up?"

"Split it up?" Rusty asked. "We could hardly open the dumb thing."

"I mean whatever's inside."

Chet thought for a second. "Whatever it is, we can't keep it."

"How do you figure?"

"If it's money, it has to go back to the owner."

"Did your brain freeze up here?" Eddy asked.

"I just think that with all the police, it must be stolen."

Eddy took a deep breath and looked at his friends. "Sometimes you guys really tick me off. I say we look. Then we can decide." He turned back to the case and slowly began lifting the top. As light from the oil lamp pierced the darkness of the case all three boys saw it at the same time and all three boys whistled.

"I've never seen that much money in one place in my whole life . . . ever," Eddy grunted.

"Including Monopoly," Rusty added.

"Man," Eddy continued. "We . . . are . . . rich!"

"We are not," Chet challenged.

"How come?"

"Because we can't keep it."

"Now hold on a second, Chester Do Right," Eddy mocked. "I happen to know that we *can* keep it."

"How?"

"Because possession is nine-tenths of the law."

"Nine what?" Rusty asked.

"Nine-tenths. It's like this. If you lost a dollar and I found it, I get to keep it. Finders, keepers, that's what I always say."

"Where'd you get that idea?" Chet asked.

"My uncle's a lawyer. He told me that if you find something, the real owner has to prove it belongs to him. So with that dollar, it's like ninety cents of it is mine and you only have ten. You have to prove you're the owner. Anyway, the insurance company might take a hit, but they have plenty of money."

"It still doesn't sound right to me," Chet scolded.

"We can use the money to go to college or buy a car when we turn sixteen. Plus, do you really believe those guys would take a chance coming back here? Even if they did get away from the police, we'll be back home safe in our beds. There's no way they could ever find us."

"Yeah," Rusty said as he nodded his approval.

"Even if they did come back here, I don't think they'd walk up, knock on our front door, and say, 'Excuse me, boys. Did you happen to find a silver case in the back yard, filled with cash? We threw it over your fence when the police were chasing us.'"

"But . . . it didn't belong to them," Chet said

"Sure it did. They had possession. Get it?"

"You've got it all turned around, Eddy. You can't keep something that was stolen from somebody else in the first place. It's cheating."

"Oh," Rusty interrupted, "now I see why Eddy thinks he should get to keep it."

"Don't start with me, Russ. I'm warning you. When my dad gets back, we can ask him. It's his cabin, it was his back yard, and I think he'll say it's his case too."

"His case?" Rusty asked.

"That didn't come out right. We don't have to tell him about the money. We can just ask, so he won't know. You guys leave it to me. For now we have to hide this thing again. I know a place up in the rafters."

The boys hurried upstairs and hid the case. Later their fathers came back from fishing.

"Don't say a word about the money," Eddy warned.

Chapter 8

The cough drops took care of whatever had been bothering Eddy's father. He cooked another one of his famous dinners. This time he roasted whole chickens on a metal bar in the fireplace. He wrapped potatoes in aluminum foil and buried them in the hot coals. The scent of fresh biscuits filled the cabin while a pot of mixed vegetables boiled on the stove.

Rusty stuck his nose up and sniffed the air. "I don't ever want to go home again. You make the best food."

"Better not let your mother hear you say that," his father cautioned.

"I know, but it's true." Realizing what he had said, Rusty quickly covered his mouth with both hands.

The boys gulped their food as usual, but Eddy could tell they had their minds on the silver case, wondering what was going to happen to all that cash. After dinner, they ate peach pie with vanilla ice cream on top.

"Man, I am *stuffed*," Chet groaned.

"Me, too," Rusty added.

"Hey, Dad," Eddy began, "I gotta ask you something."

"Sure, what is it?"

"Well . . . suppose a guy found something that belonged to somebody else."

"Like what?"

"That part's not important. Just suppose."

"I don't know. Where did this guy find whatever it is he found?"

"What if it was right in his own back yard?"

"Well, then I guess he could keep it."

Eddy turned and just grinned at his friends. Without making a sound he moved his mouth to say, "Told you so."

"I have a question," Chet's father said. "If it was something like a dog, and the dog had a collar, and the collar had an address, what then?"

"Or what if it was a letter that blew into your yard from your neighbor's house, and it had a check inside?" Rusty's father asked.

Eddy jammed his hands into his pockets in disgust. "You guys are making this way too complicated. It isn't a dog. There's no collar with an address. And it is definitely not a letter from next door. Come on, we don't even have a next door out here."

"Out here?" Chet's father asked.

"Forget I said that," Eddy grumbled.

"Well, then," Eddy's father began, "you know what Uncle Nick always says."

Eddy blurted out, "Yeah, possession is nine-tenths of the law."

"You remember that?"

"I remember lots of thing you and Uncle Nick tell me."

"Now, *there's* something that's always bothered me," Chet's father said. "I mean, if you know it isn't yours, and you know it truly belongs to someone else, isn't that kind of like cheating the other person?"

"They shouldn't have been dumb enough to throw it over the fence then," Eddy fumed.

"Just what is it we're talking about here?" his father demanded.

Chet looked over at Eddy. "You might as well go up and get it."

Now, Eddy was truly angry. His face turned bright red. Anytime he had an argument about right and wrong with Chet, it always made him feel guilty. Eddy slowly stood up and went to get the case from its hiding place.

When he came back into the room, he just shook his head. "You guys aren't gonna believe this." He placed the case in the middle of the coffee table and opened it.

"Oh, man!" Rusty's father gasped. "There must be thousands."

"Two hundred and fifty thousand to be exact," Eddy reported. "We counted it this afternoon."

"Well, where did it come from?" his father asked.

"Right out of heaven . . . sort of," Eddy answered.

"It did not," Chet grumbled.

The boys proceeded to tell their fathers the whole story about watching Stupid and Stupider through the fence, the police, and everything.

After they finished, Chet's father said, "There's only one thing we can do."

"What's that?" Eddy's father asked.

"It has to go back."

"Back where?" Eddy demanded. "To who?"

"We have to turn it in."

"Who put you in charge?" Eddy asked. "This is our cabin."

"He's right," Rusty's father said. "We're going to have to take it to the police. There could be a reward."

Eddy laughed, "A reward? A *reward*? I think the best reward is to keep all of it."

Sternly Chet's father replied, "Well, you can't do that."

"Why not?" Eddy pleaded.

"If it's from a robbery, there are laws about it. And if it's drug money . . . well, it can go to help fight crime."

Eddy's father stood and tapped his finger to his chin. "I'm afraid I have to agree with them, son."

"Dad! Of all people, I can't believe you'd say anything like that."

"That's just the way it is."

The group continued to discuss and argue, argue and discuss until far into the night. Finally, they decided to take a vote.

"Majority rules," Chet's father announced. "All in favor of turning in the money, raise your hands."

Everyone did except Eddy.

"All in favor of keeping it, raise your hands," Eddy begged. But his was the only hand in the air.

After breakfast the next morning, Eddy's father slipped the case into a large, black garbage bag. When they walked out the door, everyone noticed how cold the weather had turned.

Giving back the money made Eddy feel even colder. "I can't believe we're doing this," he complained.

It took forty-five minutes to drive to the rural police department. All the way there, Eddy worried about someone stealing the money, so he sat on it. He looked pretty funny with his head almost sticking through the roof, and it was nearly impossible to fasten his seatbelt. When they finally pulled into the parking lot of the station, Eddy's heart started pounding.

"I really hate giving it back," he complained.

After they went inside, Eddy's father explained what had happened. A police officer gave him a stack of forms to fill out.

"Yeah," the officer told them, "we chased those guys across three counties, but we lost them on the main road. They must have been a couple of really smart ones."

"No, sir," Eddy said. "They were as dumb as a box of rocks."

The officer laughed, "That might be, son, but they got away from us."

"Didn't anyone catch them?" Chet's father asked.

"For all we know, they could be clean across the country by now. We had a description of them and their car sent out to police in neighboring states."

"A big shiny four-wheel-drive beauty, right?" Rusty asked.

"No, I don't think so. Let me look at the sheet on those two." The officer went to his file and pulled out some papers. "Says here that they ditched the fancy truck and stole an old rusted dark blue van from a farm not too far from here."

Eddy shook his head. "I don't get it. They had all that money, and what did they do? Threw it over a fence. Then they gave up a new truck for some heap."

"The new one was probably stolen, too," Chet suggested.

The police officer scratched his head. "I'm not sure if this will make any sense to you, but I've met quite a few criminals in my time. When they steal something, it has no real value to them. The way they think is it'll be easy to steal something else around the next corner. Some crooks even cheat on each other. Or worse."

Eddy thought about that. *What would it be like if I couldn't trust anybody?* he wondered.

After they got back to the cabin, he decided to talk with Chet. While Rusty and his dad played a board game, the two boys put on warm clothes and slipped out to the snow fort. They each took a crate and sat down.

"What did you bring me out here for?" Chet asked. "It's freezing."

"I know, but I needed to talk with you . . . private."

"What about?"

"All everybody thinks I am . . . is a big cheater."

"You are a big cheater, Eddy."

"I know, but everyone I know cheats."

"I don't."

"No, I mean in my family. How come you don't?"

"My dad explained it to me in a way I never forgot. I had gotten some extra stuff in my bag when I went to the store once. There I was bragging about it when he said, 'How would you like it if you owned the store, and people walked out with things they didn't pay for . . . things that belonged to *you* and cost *you* money?'"

"Yeah," Eddy broke in, "I hate it when I get ripped off. I watch you, Chet. You never lie. You don't steal. How come you're so different?"

"Because my dad told me something else. He said we always have choices. Everybody has choices. He told me even Jesus had a choice. He even prayed and asked God to change things. He could have changed his mind or made excuses. He could have even tried too let someone else die. But he didn't."

"Why not?"

"He was the only one who could do it."

"So why did he? Die, I mean?"

"Jesus could have cheated. He could have decided not to die."

"But. . . ." Eddy stammered.

"That was all part of God's plan. Jesus died to cover up our sins."

"I like that. Then I can do anything I want and not feel bad about it."

"No, you can't. When you accept who Jesus really is, then something inside of you changes. You don't even want to do some of the bad stuff anymore."

"How come?"

"I can't explain it. You'd have to see how it feels for yourself. I mean, I wouldn't even know the right words."

"How can a guy . . . I mean . . . could I. . . ."

"All I can do is tell you how it was for me."

Eddy continued listening.

"I just told Jesus I was sorry for the bad things I like to do. I asked him to forgive me and to be in charge of my life."

"Really? And he did that?"

"Still does . . . every day."

"Man . . . but I'd feel kind of goofy doing that out here in a snow fort."

"It doesn't matter where you are. You can do it all by yourself, if you want to, later. Just make sure you honestly believe Jesus is who he said he is. Ask him to come in. Tell him you need him to clean up your life. Promise to trust him every day to help you."

"That's all?"

"That's it."

"I'll do it . . . only not out here. On my own, later."

"Great. But would you do one more thing?"

"I knew there must be a catch."

"No catch. I'd just like you to tell me if you do it. Okay?"

"I guess so."

The boys walked back to the cabin. When they went in, Rusty asked, "Where you guys been?"

"We just went out to work on the . . ." then Eddy stopped himself. "We went out to talk. That's all."

"About what?"

"We talked. Okay?"

"You don't need to get so touchy about it."

"Well, boys," Eddy's father announced, "tomorrow we have to pack this place up and head back home."

"Aw . . ." the boys groaned. "Do we have to?"

"Your mothers are going to be so happy to see you all again," Chet's father told them.

Later, as Eddy lay in his bed, his mind raced from one thought to another. *Could Jesus really do what Chet told me? Where were the crooks? Would there be a reward? What if those scary men come back in the night while we're still here sleeping?* he worried. That gave him a shiver. He pulled the covers up around his neck. *I sure hope they don't,* he thought.

Chapter 9

When morning came, Eddy was relieved that he was still alive. The men hadn't come back, and he felt safe. He heard voices out in the kitchen. When he walked out there, his father was making waffles while others began packing for the trip home.

"I'm kinda sad we have to leave," he told his father.

"We've had a great time. That's for sure. Sit down and have something to eat."

Rusty came in from taking a load to the truck. "I'm going to miss that cool snow fort we built. Wish we could take it home with us. The guys at school would never believe it."

Before noon the floors were swept, the truck was loaded, and Eddy's father locked the cabin door.

"We should come up here every winter," Eddy told him.

"You mean all of us?"

"Sure. Why not?"

"I'll think about it," his father said.

Eddy could tell that no one wanted to leave. For the first hour on the trip home, they didn't say anything. Then Rusty asked, "Do you think we'll get a reward?"

"The police officer told me the money *did* come from a bank. He gave me all the information," Eddy's father answered.

"Wow! We might still be rich," Rusty said.

"Hey, Dad," Eddy called out. "Do you think I could have the guys over one more time before school starts?"

"You mean for an overnight?"

"Yeah."

"Well, tomorrow night us parents are going out for New Year's Eve. You could do it then."

"That's a great idea," Rusty agreed.

A light snow started falling. Heavy wind blew it across the road. Before long, small drifts began forming. The light snow turned heavier and the wind blew even harder, making it nearly impossible to see the road anymore. Hidden beneath the blowing snow were larger drifts on the roadway.

Without warning, Eddy's father hit one, turning the truck sideways. He fought hard to regain control, but the truck left the road and careened into the median.

"I don't want to get stuck in here," he said as he pushed the gas peddle to the floor. Even though the engine was at full power, their big lumbering truck seemed to move in slow motion. As they continued through the center strip between the divided Interstate, their front end acted like a snow blower. Powdered snow flew up over the front of the truck completely covering the windshield. Finally, they felt the truck level off again.

"Don't ask me how, but I think we're back on the road," Eddy's father shouted. Everyone else cheered and whistled. But when he turned on his windshield wipers their excitement turned to terror.

"Dad! Do something!" Eddy screamed.

Heading straight toward them was a giant eighteen-wheeler with its brights on. The trucker blew his horn and locked the brakes. Eddy's father hit the gas and that diesel-belching monster only missed them by a paint job.

"Thank you, Lord," Chet's father said right out loud.

Eddy's father laughed. "Thank you, SUV."

They quickly found a place to go back across to the other side of the Interstate. From then on, Eddy's father kept the truck in four-wheel drive and drove a lot slower.

After they returned home, Eddy didn't think about the money very much. There was another battle going on in his mind. *I wonder if what Chet told me is true?* he questioned himself. He felt safe back home, too. *Those guys could never find us in a million years,* he thought. *Besides, it's New Year's Eve.*

Eddy's parents, along with Chet's and Rusty's were going out to dinner and then to a New Year's Eve party. They didn't plan to be back before at least two o'clock in the morning.

Eddy's mother made lots of goodies for the boys to eat. They had bags of popcorn, chips and salsa, crackers, ice cream, and a table full of other good food.

The other parents brought their boys over to Eddy's. They'd leave their cars, ride to the party together, and then come back to pick up their sons later.

"You boys be good," Rusty's mother warned.

Chet's father laughed. "Don't burn the house down or anything."

"Nothing to worry about," Eddy told them. "We couldn't be in a safer place."

Chet and Rusty brought their best video games over. Eddy's parents rented some DVDs, and Chet's mother bought noisemakers and hats for the boys.

"No way we're wearing those dumb hats," Eddy whispered.

"I know," Chet answered. "I tried to tell her we didn't need them."

After the parents left, the boys played video games till they thought their eyes would fall out on the floor.

"Let's eat something," Eddy suggested.

They proceeded to stuff themselves. As far as Eddy was concerned, the cabin and those scary crooks were gone forever. He figured the money was gone, too.

After eating they watched a couple cartoon movies. Then they decided to go into the basement and play pool and ping-pong in the rec room. Eddy's father had two old pinball machines standing along one wall. "Can we try those?" Rusty asked.

"Why not?"

That kept them busy for the next hour. "Real games can be as much fun as video games," Chet noted.

"Even funner," Rusty said.

Finally, they were tired of playing any games that made them stand up. "You guys want to watch movies?" Eddy asked.

"What have you got?" Chet wanted to know.

"A couple monsters, an old gangster movie about bank robbers, and a western."

"Let's watch the bank robbers," Rusty said.

"Does it have Dillenger in it?" Chet asked.

"It might," Eddy called over his shoulder as he ran for the stairs. "Last one up is a bugger!"

"I don't wanna be a bugger," Rusty cried. Then he slipped on a rug and fell.

"Bugger, bugger, bugger," Eddy hollered.

"You cut that out," Rusty warned. Then he ran up the stairs, too. When he got to the family room, Eddy was already slipping the DVD into the machine. "We can crank the sound up real loud, too," he said with a smile.

The movie was an old black and white. When the robbers started shooting up banks and stealing money, it reminded Eddy of the two crooks he'd seen at the cabin. He thought about how it wasn't right to take money that didn't belong to him. He was now actually glad they had turned it in.

After the movie was over, Eddy took a few dishes to the kitchen. Rusty started playing another video game, so Chet went to help Eddy. When Chet came into the kitchen, Eddy turned and said, "I want to tell you something."

"What?"

"The thing you told me to do . . . when we were out in the fort."

"What thing was that?"

Eddy took a deep breath. "Man, do you have to make this so hard?"

"Ohhhh!" Chet exclaimed. "Now I get it."

"Well, I just wanted you to know that I . . . I did what

you said."

"That is so great, Eddy. You know what this means, don't you?"

"What?"

"It means we're brothers now."

"Brothers?"

"Sure. In God's family, I mean."

"I never had a brother before."

"Well, now you do."

"Hey, you guys," Rusty called from the other room. "Come see this. I'm on level ten."

The boys hurried out to see because Rusty was the best video game player of the group. The highest Chet and Eddy could get to on this game was level five.

"Rusty, you are the man," Chet told him.

"Yeah, but I'm bored. You got any more movies?" he asked.

Eddy pulled another DVD from the pile. "I thought we could try this one. Last time I saw it, it scared me half to death."

"Let's see if it can finish the job when you watch it again."

"Ha . . . ha . . . ha . . . Russ."

"For this one we have to turn the lights real dim. I'm telling you. You're gonna freak out."

Eddy kept his eye on his friends as the movie started. Spooky music played over the first dark scene in a swamp. It was night, and a thick fog drifted across the still, black water. A sound effect of a heartbeat started thumping louder and louder. Chet and Rusty scrunched down deeper into the couch cushions until just their heads and shoulders stuck out. They each held on to a big pillow across their chests as if that might protect them from the monsters.

Then it happened.

A dark form lumbered into the picture, stopped for a moment, and then moved off into the swamp.

"What was that?" Eddy asked in a loud whisper.

Chet and Rusty practically jumped out of the couch.

"Cut it out," Rusty complained.

"That wasn't funny," Chet added.

In a deeper whisper, Eddy said, "No, honest. I am not kidding, I *really* heard something.

"Just quit it, okay? Rusty begged.

Suddenly the TV went off. So did every light in the house. They heard a loud thump outside.

"Somebody's out there," Eddy growled.

Chapter 10

"Whada we do?" Rusty whispered.

"Call 911," Chet suggested.

Eddy picked up the phone, but just as he did that, it went dead. "They cut the line."

"Who did?" Rusty asked.

"I don't know. Just somebody!"

"Well, who would want to do that?" Rusty demanded.

"How should I know?"

"Doesn't your dad have a cell phone?" Chet asked.

"He does, but it's always with him. He uses it mostly for his business."

The boys huddled in the darkness trying to decide what they should do next. No one said a word. The only sounds were their breathing and a grandfather clock in the hallway.

Just then it struck once, reminding them that they had forgotten all about midnight.

"Happy New Year," Eddy whispered.

"Not really," Rusty answered. "We gotta do something."

"Like what?" Eddy asked.

"I don't know . . . something . . . anything."

Eddy had an idea. "You guys stay here. I'm gonna check something." He got down flat on the floor and slithered like a snake across the room. Then he was out of sight. He continued down the hall in the darkness until he ran into a small table. A glass vase with fake flowers teetered, then fell to the floor, crashing into a million pieces.

"What was that?" Rusty asked in a hoarse voice.

"It was nothing. Be quiet." Eddy called back. He continued down the hall and into the living room. There he moved toward the picture window looking out over the street in front of his house. He had to crawl around behind the couch, and when he reached the window, he slowly rose up, pulled open the curtains, and looked out.

What he saw made him choke. For a moment he couldn't take a breath. At first, it felt like he might pass right out, but he didn't. He ducked down again to think. Slowly, he rose up one more time to make sure. There was no mistake.

Eddy turned and crawled all the way back to the

room where his friends waited in the dark.

As he came nearer, Chet whispered, "Eddy, is that you?"

"Yes," was the response. Quickly he crawled up to them.

"See anything?" Rusty asked.

"Boy, did I ever."

"What . . . was it?" Chet asked.

"A dark blue, rusty van is parked right out front."

"Oh, please, no," Rusty cried.

"How did they find us?" Chet asked. "And on the one night we're together without any parents."

"Maybe they aren't as dumb as we thought."

"I didn't think the driver was dumb at all," Chet said.

"We should go down and hide in the basement," Eddy suggested.

Defiantly, Rusty said, "No way. I've seen a lot of scary movies and the last place you want to go is in the basement."

"What difference does it make?" Eddy asked.

"In the movies, people always die in the basement."

"But this isn't a movie," Chet reminded him. "This is real life."

"I know. If it *was* a movie, I'd be the first one to turn the thing off."

"So what then?" Chet asked.

"I say we go up," Rusty suggested. "Up is always better than down."

Then the boys heard the sound of glass breaking downstairs.

Rusty folded his arms across his chest. "See. What'd I tell you?"

"The door down to the basement has a lock," Eddy told them. "If we can get there first, they can't come up."

They rushed just in time to bolt the door. The boys heard footsteps on the stairs leading up from the basement.

"We know you're there, boys," a low voice warned, "and we're coming up."

A wave of courage swept over Eddy. "Who are you? And what do you want?"

"Oh, dat's a good one, ain't it, Boss?"

Now, there was no doubt. Somehow the crooks had followed them back to their home town. How else could they know where Eddy lived?

The other man spoke. "All we want is the money, and we'll be on our way."

"What money?"

"Dem kids is makin' me mad, Boss."

"Shut up. You talk too much."

Eddy crept over to the sink. He quietly filled a large pot with water and put it on the gas stove. Then he turned the flame up all the way to high.

"You seem like nice boys. Give us the money, and we'll leave you alone."

Eddy heard the grandfather clock chime the quarter hour. *Great,* he thought. *Our parents won't be back for nearly an hour.*

"I don't want to hafta break down this nice door, but I will if you make me."

Eddy wanted to keep them talking until the water got good and hot. "Why do you think we have any money that belongs to you?"

"Easy. You were up at the cabin."

"Are you saying you *saw* us up there?"

"No, we didn't see anyone."

"So, I don't get it," Eddy continued.

"We threw the money over the fence because the cops was chasing us. But when we came back, it was gone."

"Maybe someone else found it."

"I don't tink so," the other man said.

"I told you to shut up."

Eddy looked over to the pot which was up to full boil already. "So, how did you find us?"

"That was the easy part. We just went into town, walked right into the courthouse there in Michigan, and looked up who owned the cabin. And what do you think?"

"What?" Eddy asked as he moved over to get the pot.

"Your daddy's name came up and this address. Now ain't that interesting?"

Eddy grabbed a couple of potholders and took the boiling water off the stove. He crept back to the basement door. "Well, I guess I have to *give it to you* then."

"Now, you're gettin' smart, kid."

"If I give you what you want, you'll leave?"

"I promise."

Eddy eased the pot up to the bottom of the door. "Here you go then." He tipped it over and scalding hot water poured under the door and cascaded down the steps.

"Eeeeyowww," two voices screamed. It sounded like a couple of bowling balls bouncing down the stairs. For a few seconds after that, there was silence.

"You shouldn't odda done dat, kid."

"Will . . . you . . . get . . . off me," the other man grunted.

"We'd better get upstairs," Eddy whispered. "Those guys are going to be really mad."

"Gonna be?" Rusty snickered.

The boys scampered to the upstairs part of the house. As they reached the top step, they heard the basement door crash in.

"It wouldn't hurt to pray, too. Would it?" Eddy asked.

Rusty came to an abrupt stop. "What did you say?"

"You heard me."

"You're right, Eddy. It wouldn't hurt," Chet said.

"Could we do it right now?"

Chet smiled. "Sure. Dear Lord, we're in big trouble here. Please help us figure out the right thing to do. Please, Lord. Thank you. Amen."

"We can go to my parents' bathroom. It has two doors. One of them leads to a stairway back to the kitchen. It's got a window, in case we want to climb out on the roof."

Rusty squinted his eyes. "You're kidding, right?"

"Follow me," Eddy ordered.

The boys could already hear heavy footsteps down on the kitchen floor. Quickly they headed for the master bathroom. Once inside, Eddy locked the door to the bedroom. Then he locked the other door leading downstairs.

"What now?" Rusty asked.

"Now we wait."

"Wait for what?"

"I'm thinking," Eddy told him. He sat on the edge of the hot tub when something caught his eye. "I can't believe it."

"Believe what?" Chet asked.

"My dad never goes anywhere without his phone."

"I know," Rusty sighed. "You told us."

Eddy pointed. "Yeah, but look over there on the counter."

The boys looked where he pointed. "Are you sure it isn't his electric razor?" Rusty asked.

"Dead sure. He always charges the phone right there. He must have either forgot it or decided he didn't need it at the party."

"Well, let's use it." Rusty said.

"You can call 911 on a cell, can't you?" Chet asked.

"Yes, you can." Eddy reached for the phone, turned it on, and punched in the numbers. Then he hit send. The phone started ringing. A woman's voice on the other end said, "911. What is your emergency?"

"Please don't hang up," Eddy pleaded. "This isn't a joke."

"How can I help you?" she asked.

"My name is Eddy Thompson. I live at 720 North Lake Street. It's a long story. Where should I start?"

"What's the emergency?" she repeated.

"Two men have broken into my house. I have my friends with me, but all our parents are at a New Year's Eve party. What should we do?"

"Stay on the line with me," she ordered. "Don't hang up."

"Okay."

"Where are you now, and where are these men?"

"We're upstairs in my parents' bathroom. The men are downstairs, but they're looking for us. Please, could you send someone? Hurry!"

"I've already dispatched two squad cars to your location."

"Listen," Eddy warned. "You can't just send Barney out here with his one bullet. These guys are dangerous. They followed us all the way from our cabin in Michigan. You'd better send out the army or something."

"What do you know about them?"

"They robbed a bank up in Michigan. We took their money, but we turned it in to the police up there. Now they think we still have it. Listen, you'd better send a lot of police and make sure they come with their sirens and lights off, or these guys will just run away."

"You're a smart boy. Do you know what kind of car they're driving?"

"It's an old rusty, blue van," Eddy's voice began to quiver. "Please hurry, I can hear them coming up the stairs. Please!"

Chapter 11

"Just stay calm," the 911 operator said softly. "Our officers should be in your neighborhood any minute."

Eddy heard the two men moving through the hallway as they opened the door to each room, checked inside, then moved on to the next. From under the door he noticed beams from flashlights the men carried.

"Dey ain't up here no place," one of them said.

"Keep looking."

"Is there anyplace you can hide?" the woman asked.

"There are two ways out of this bathroom. One takes us down a back stairway to the kitchen."

"Can you go that way?"

"I think so."

"Where could you hide in the kitchen?

"We have a big closet where my mom keeps food and stuff. It has a bunch of shelves."

"Go there. I'll tell the officers that's where you'll be.

Keep your phone on and tell me when you get down there."

The boys eased over to the door. Eddy unlocked it and opened the door to the stairs. As they slipped out of the bathroom, Eddy heard the other doorknob turn. Someone jiggled it several times. Just as he closed the door behind him, Eddy heard one of the men say, "Bust it down."

There were three loud crunches and one big crash. The boys hurried down the stairs, through the kitchen, and into the closet.

"Could you make it a little darker in here, because I can't see a thing," Rusty complained. Then he bumped into a plastic bucket and knocked it over.

"Shhh," Chet warned.

"Sorry," Rusty whispered.

The boys crouched down and stacked as many things in front of them as they could find in the dark.

Eddy got back on the phone. "We made it," he told the woman. But there was no response. "I said we made it . . . over."

"It's a phone, not a radio," Rusty snickered.

"The battery's dead. That must be why my dad left it behind. Now, all we can do is wait. At least they're supposed to know where we are."

"Yeah," Rusty whined, "but what if she wanted to tell us, 'You've got ten seconds. They're gonna gas the place.

Run for your life?'"

"I really wish you wouldn't say things like that," Chet scolded.

"Quiet," Eddy warned. "Someone's coming down the stairs."

The boys listened as the steps creaked. The men from upstairs were definitely on their way down.

I wish this dumb cell phone worked, Eddy thought. Once again he turned it on, just to see. The face lit up like sunshine. Eddy quickly dialed 911, but before he could hit the send button, the screen went black. "Lousy battery," he whispered.

Second by agonizing second Eddy heard the men coming closer.

"They don't know where we are," Rusty whispered with a nervous laugh.

"We should have gone outside when we had the chance," Chet added.

"The 911 lady told us to stay in here."

Rusty let out a heavy breath. "Yeah, but she's safe in a warm office with lights and everything. And we're . . ."

The footsteps sounded on the kitchen floor. At least Eddy knew it was dark for the men, too, except for their flashlights. *Maybe they'll think we left,* he thought. He didn't even realize it but as he began to pray, he was actually whispering. His friends listened as he said, "God, I know I'm kinda new at this. And you might not even know me yet. This is Eddy. I don't know what we should do, and I'm really scared. Please send help . . . quick. Amen."

"Amen," Chet whispered.

The men continued rattling around through the kitchen, looking in all the cabinets, slamming them shut one at a time.

Eddy felt around on the shelves and took down several cans. He handed them to his friends. "If they find us in here," Eddy instructed, "wait for my signal. When I say 'now,' you just start throwing cans as hard and as fast as you can. Got it?"

His friends whispered in the dark, "Got it."

"Then what?" Rusty asked.

"Let's head for the basement."

"Why not outside?" Chet asked.

"I told you. The police expect to find us in the house."

Suddenly, everything was quiet out in the kitchen.

Then, "I'm tellin' ya, Boss, da boys ain't here."

"And I'm telling you they are. Now keep looking. They might have seen us and know who we are. We can't leave no witnesses."

Eddy's heart started pounding so hard, he thought they would be able to find him just from the sound of it.

Then something horrible happened. The doorknob to the closet where they were hiding began turning. There was a click. The door slowly opened. Powerful beams from two flashlights blinded Eddy and his friends. They closed their eyes tightly.

Then an angry voice thundered, "I know you're in here. You might as well come on out."

"Yeah, da boss ain't kiddin'. Are ya, Boss?"

"Shut up."

"Oh, sorry."

"I said shut up."

"Okay, Boss."

"If you say one more word, I'll. . . ."

"I won't."

"You just did."

"No, Boss. Ya tol' me if I said one more word. Dat was two words."

"This is the last job we are *ever* doing together."

Then one of the lights shined right in Eddy's face.

"There you are!"

"You shouldn't odda have tossed dat hot water on us. I'm very angry bout dat."

Eddy slowly stood to his feet. "Come on guys. They've got us." Chet and Rusty stood up too. As his eyes adjusted to the light he saw the same men from the fence. Only now they were standing right in front of him in his own house.

"My parents will be home any minute. You'd better run while you can."

"That's a good one, kid. We've been watching your house, just waiting for the right time. When we were sure your parents were gone, and the three of you staying here together. . . . What a set up!"

"Well, they're coming right back," Rusty said.

"Oh? I don't think so. This is New Year's Eve. Remember?"

"So?" Eddy asked.

"They'll probably stay out all night."

"Don't bet on it."

"Okay. I'm done playing. Where is our money?"

"It isn't your money," Eddy told him.

"Not our money? You're a real comedian."

"Well, it isn't. You stole it so that means it belongs to someone else, not you," Eddy continued.

"Look, we had the money. We threw it into your yard for safe keeping."

The heavy man cleared his throat, "Um, Boss, I did dat."

"It doesn't matter who did it, stupid."

"My name's Clarence."

"What's the difference?"

"Um, Stupid is Stupid . . . and Clarence is. . . ."

"Stupid. Go look it up when you get home."

"I don't tink dat's right, Boss." He looked at Eddy and his friends. "Why ya holdin' dem cans, huh?"

The other man looked toward the ceiling. "You are *impossible*." But when he looked up, it gave Eddy the opportunity he was looking for.

"NOW!" he yelled.

"Now wha . . . ?" the heavy man asked. Only he didn't have to wait to find out. Heavy cans started flying at the men from all directions like water balloons only much harder. The men dropped their flashlights, covered their heads, and ducked.

"Let's go!" Eddy ordered.

The boys burst out of the closet with such speed, they knocked the men to the floor as if they were the defensive line on the worst team in the NFL.

"To the basement," Eddy called over his shoulder.

The boys felt their way along in the dark, holding onto the handrail all the way downstairs.

One of the flashlights broke when it hit the floor upstairs, but one didn't. The men quickly chased after the boys using the good one.

From the basement Eddy saw their light at the top of the stairs. Then he heard the sickening thump, thump,

thump as they started coming down.

"I know a place we can hide . . . behind our furnace in the storage room. We should be safe there." Eddy led his friends in that direction.

"I'm done trying to be nice to you boys. Now give me my money."

"Uh . . . don't ya mean our money, Boss?"

The other man simply growled.

The boys crawled behind some hanging storage bags Eddy's mother used to keep their summer clothes in until spring. The bags hung nearly to the floor.

"Quick! Behind here," Eddy told them. There was a space between the bags and the back wall big enough for them to hide. The flashlight kept coming closer and closer as the men finally entered the storage room. Eddy felt around on the floor until he found an old clay flowerpot. He stood up, pushed out between two of the storage bags, and hurled the pot as far as he could throw it. The pot crashed on the cement floor nearly half way across the huge dark room.

"What was dat?"

"Dat . . . you idiot, used to be a flowerpot," the other man said as his light passed over the broken pieces on the floor.

Then Eddy heard something that frightened him so

badly he slumped to the floor. Above the boys' heads, they heard several footsteps.

Oh, no, Eddy thought. "Our parents."

"What should we do?" Rusty whispered.

"We can't do anything," Eddy answered.

"He's right. If we try to warn them, those guys will find us," Chet added.

"And turn us into hostages or something."

All the boys could do was stay hidden and simply wait to see what would happen next.

This is bad. Really bad, Eddy thought.

Chapter 12

Eddy wanted to warn his parents and the others, but there was nothing he could do. If he said anything, the men would find him. If he didn't say anything, they could hurt his parents. He was just about to yell when he heard the sound of footsteps coming down the stairs into the rec room.

"Someone's comin', Boss."

"I know, you nit."

"Um . . . you mean, nit wit, don't ya?"

"You're too dumb to be called a whole name."

"They're going to hurt our parents," Rusty whispered.

"We can't let that happen," Chet added. "What do you wanna do, Eddy?"

"We might have robbed that bank, but you boys wouldn't want to cheat us out of our money. Would you? Just give us the silver case and we'll leave."

"When I count to three, let's run out of here in three different directions," Eddy said. "There's only two of them and three of us. Someone has to make it out."

Rusty swallowed hard. "Let's do it."

"One," Eddy whispered.

Whoever was on the steps was nearly to the bottom now.

"Two."

But before Eddy could say three, more flashlights than he had ever seen before, in the same place, at the same time, came on.

From the blinding lights a voice boomed, "Police! Come out with your hands up. Now!"

"Is he talking to us?" Rusty asked.

Eddy shrugged his shoulders.

"Now! I said," the officer repeated.

Slowly the two robbers walked out from the shadows. The fat man pointed to the other man. "It was all his idea. I just come along to help him steal da . . ." But he didn't finish.

"My idea? If you hadn't thrown the case over the fence. . . ."

"But ya tol me ta do dat."

"Well, you didn't have to do it."

"I didn'? I didn' know dat.

"Sometimes you are so dumb."

"You said we was partners. Dat must make us both dumb."

"Down on the floor!" the loud voice commanded. The men got down as several policemen with bullet proof vests burst into the storage room. Two of them put handcuffs on the men. Then they pulled them to their feet.

"Let's go. We have a nice warm jail cell for you two."

"Didya hear dat, Boss? A jail cell. Dat's nice."

The other man shook his head and let out a deep breath as they were taken up the stairs. Eddy heard their steps above his head as the police led the men outside. Then other footsteps came thundering in.

"Eddy . . . Chet . . . Russ . . . Where are you?" Several voices cried out all at once.

"Our parents!" Eddy yelled. The boys pushed their way out from behind the storage bags.

One of the police officers turned to look as they came out. "So that's where you boys were . . . good thinking."

The lights in the house came back on and the furnace kicked in. The boys' parents rushed down the stairs.

"What in the world is going on?" Eddy's father demanded.

"The men from the cabin, Dad. They came here tonight. They found out where we lived. I was so scared."

"We all were," Chet added.

Rusty nodded his head, "No kidding."

"After the police lost them, they went back to the cabin. When the money wasn't there, they went into town and looked up who owned the place. One of them told us they'd been watching our house waiting for the right time."

Rusty's mother shuddered. "How awful."

The mothers ran to their sons and hugged them as tight as they could.

"There's broken glass and smashed doors all over the place," Eddy's father complained.

"We'll get someone out here yet tonight and board up the broken windows," the officer assured them. "You can get new glass put in tomorrow."

"But it's New Years Day."

"It is, isn't it? Well, the next day then."

Eddy's mother fumed, "I have to go through the entire day with our neighbors looking at boarded up windows. It's so embarrassing!"

"Happy New Year," Rusty said sarcastically. The parents started laughing. That made the boys laugh, and when they did, some of the police did too.

"One thing is good," the officer told them.

"What could possibly be good about it?" Eddy's father demanded.

"You did the right thing. You turned in the money.

Some people might have tried to keep it."

"I'm not so sure that was such a good thing."

"But when you did that, the case was dusted for fingerprints. There were a lot of them that couldn't be identified."

"I think those were ours," Eddy said.

"You're probably right about that. But both of theirs were on it, too."

"How did you know who they belonged to?"

"There's a big computer file with all the known prints stored in it. It didn't take long until a match was found. Once that was done, we knew who we were dealing with."

"So who are they?" Chet asked.

"A couple of small-time operators. This bank robbery was their biggest score yet. I think it even surprised *them*. But our records also showed they would never hurt anyone. They don't even use guns."

"You mean . . .?" Eddy asked.

"You boys were never in any real serious danger."

"Well, it felt pretty serious to us," Rusty said.

"We knew they were in the area because we'd traced the stolen van. One of my officers saw it parked on your street tonight. When you called 911, we had already seen them enter your house."

"You *let* them destroy my house?" Eddy's mother

cried. "How could you?"

"It was the only way. Since they tossed the case over your fence up in Michigan, we didn't have any hard evidence on them."

"But the fingerprints?" Rusty asked.

"That only meant they had touched the outside of the case. You boys did, too. Does that mean you're all bank robbers?"

"Well, no," Chet said, "but you almost let them get a hold of us."

"Not really. We were ready to pounce on them any second."

"So why did you wait?" Eddy asked.

The officer snapped his fingers. "Murphy, come here a minute."

Another police officer walked forward and handed him a small, dark object. The first officer held it up, pushed a red button, and the boys heard, "*We might have robbed that bank, but you boys wouldn't want to cheat us out of our money. Would you? Just give us the silver case and we'll leave.*"

"That is *so* cool," Eddy said. "What a way to catch a couple of cheaters."

Soon the police left the house. A few minutes after they drove off, Eddy looked out the front window as a tow truck pulled in front of the rusted van and prepared to haul it away. At about the same time a white cargo van pulled into the driveway. Two men stepped out, went to the back, and took out big pieces of plywood. They grabbed hammers and headed toward the broken windows.

With the sound of hammers in the distance, Eddy's father said, "Why don't you boys go on home and try to get a little sleep. You all can come back later after I figure out what to do next."

"Next?" Eddy asked.

"About the reward."

Eddy looked back at his father. "Reward? Oh, yeah, I almost forgot."

Chapter 13

When Eddy awakened the next morning, he wondered if it had been another one of his bad dreams. All he had to do was go back downstairs to see it hadn't been. His mother did her best to clean things up, but there were smashed doors and boarded up windows.

"I'm sorry those guys messed up the house, Mom."

She smiled back at him. "At least you and your friends are okay. I guess that's all that really matters." She turned to go back to her work when she remembered something.

"Oh, Chet called. He wanted to talk to you when you got up."

Eddy looked at the kitchen clock. "It's only 8:15. I wonder how he woke up so early."

"He said something about shoveling snow."

Eddy went to the wall phone and called.

"Hello," Chet answered.

"Hey, Chet. Eddy here. What's up?"

"It snowed pretty hard after we left your house last night. I was wondering if you wanted to go shovel driveways in the neighborhood. We could make a bunch of money if we did."

"Why bother?"

"What do you mean?"

"I mean, since we're expecting such a fat reward, who needs to work that hard?"

"We don't know what's going to happen. Anyway, I already called Rusty. He's coming over in about fifteen minutes. You wanna come, too?"

"I guess."

"See you when you get here."

Eddy snarfed his breakfast like it was a speed eating contest. "Mom," he said, "I'm going over to Chet's. Rusty's coming, too. We're gonna shovel snow and make some money."

His mother glanced out the window. "Looks like a good morning for it."

By the time Eddy pulled on his snowmobile suit, gloves, double socks, and heavy boots, he could hardly walk. "I feel like a robot," he told his mother.

"At least you'll be warm. Have a good time."

"Mom, we're going to be shoveling hundreds of pounds of wet snow. Who could have fun doing that?"

"Well, be careful then."

"I will."

By the time Eddy lumbered over to his friend's house, Chet and Rusty were already on the porch ready to get started.

"Where's your shovel?" Chet asked.

"With all the stuff I have on, I wasn't about to drag that clear over here, too. You got an extra?"

"I think so."

Soon the boys were standing in front of a house with one of the longest driveways in Chet's whole neighborhood.

"What do we do?" Rusty asked. "Go up to the door and ask for the money?"

"No," Eddy snickered. "That would give them a chance to say no."

"We could do the job first and then see how much they want to pay us," Rusty suggested.

Chet looked down the long driveway again. "Let's get started."

It took the boys over two hours to clear all the snow. Several times they needed to stop and rest. All three of them had to open their snowmobile suits to let in a little cool air. When they finally finished, the boys sat on a pile of snow.

Eddy took a deep breath. "I'm sweating like a pig."

"Me, too," Chet laughed. "Let's go see how much money we made." They dragged their feet up the steps to the front door. Eddy reached out to ring the bell, but the stubby fingers on his heavy gloves made it impossible to press the button. He grabbed the end of his glove between his teeth and pulled it off his hand. Then he rang the bell.

"What if no one's home?" Rusty asked.

Chet and Eddy turned and gave him an evil look. "Don't even think a thing like that," Eddy warned. Then he rang the bell again. On the third try, he said, "Someone's coming."

They heard the lock turn. A man with short white hair and a neatly trimmed mustache opened the door. He held his newspaper in one hand and simply looked out at these three strangers on his front steps. "May I help you?"

"You sure can," Rusty said. "We just shoveled your whole driveway, and we're wondering how much money you'd like to give us."

The man stretched his head out the door and looked to one side of his house. But the place where he looked was still completely covered with snow. Then he turned and looked at the clean driveway on the other side of his house. Then he started to laugh. First it was a little snort. Then he laughed harder and harder until he had to sit down, right on the freezing porch.

"What's wrong, mister?" Chet asked.

By now the man had tears streaming down his face. He still couldn't say anything. After a couple minutes of this he managed to catch his breath, wipe the tears from his face, and barely squeak, "It's . . . it's not my driveway." He pointed to the snow-covered side of his house. "That's *my* driveway."

Now the boys sank to the porch and sat in front of the man.

"Tell you what," he said. "I'll pay you boys fifteen dollars each if you do clear my driveway."

"But what about this one?" Rusty asked, pointing to the other side of the house.

"She's a nice lady, the woman who lives there. I'm sure you can explain what happened."

Eddy and his friends worked to clear the second driveway. About half way back Eddy said, "Who had the great idea to shovel first and ask questions later?"

Rusty continued shoveling as if he hadn't heard the question. Eddy tapped Chet on the shoulder, and then pointed to the snow on the ground. He stuck his shovel in a drift and leaned down to make an enormous snowball.

Chet nodded his head and made one, too. They crept up behind Rusty who continued shoveling like a city snowplow. Without warning the boys pelted their friend.

"Hey," Rusty complained. Then he dropped his shovel and the battle was on. It was every man for himself. The boys launched snowballs as quickly as they could make them. After a few minutes of tough warfare, they plopped down in the snow completely out of breath.

Chet continued breathing hard as he said, "I don't have enough energy for this after all that shoveling."

"Me neither," Rusty agreed.

After resting for a few more minutes, Eddy turned to Chet. "That was pretty scary last night."

"No kidding. Did your house get cleaned up yet?"

"It did . . . except for the stuff that gets fixed tomorrow."

"You mean the doors and windows?" Rusty asked.

Eddy nodded his head. "I wanted you to know, Chet, that I really did what you said."

"Did what?" Rusty asked.

"Eddy's a Christian now," Chet told him.

"No way."

"Russ!"

"Oh, I didn't mean it like that. I'm just surprised, that's all." Then he thought for a moment. "Eddy . . . who would have thought?"

"God can change anybody . . . if they ask Him to," Chet said.

"And I did that."

Chet looked at his friend. "I can already tell the difference."

"You can? How?"

"I just can."

Then the boys noticed that their snowball episode had scattered snow all over the section they had already shoveled. They worked quickly to finish the job. This time when they went to the door, the man was happy to pay them.

The lady next door gave them the same exact amount for her driveway. After thanking her, they walked back to the sidewalk.

Rusty looked at the money in his hand. "I wonder how she knew what to pay us?"

"I'll bet that man called her," Chet suggested.

"I've about had it for one day," Eddy groaned. "Let's go back to my house."

Rusty came to a stop. "After last night, I don't know."

"It's daylight now," Chet reminded him.

"Oh, yeah. I guess it is."

They shuffled off, slowly dragging their shovels behind them.

"You should come to Sunday school with us this week," Chet said.

"I think you'd like it," Rusty added.

"Man, I sure am glad that Jesus wasn't a cheater," Eddy told them.

Chapter 14

Christmas break seemed to be over much too quickly.
Eddy didn't see how it was possible, yet there he was, back
in school again. *How could my break be over so soon*, he
wondered. He had dreaded this day but not because school
started again. Eddy knew he had to do something. At the
end of history class, he went to see Mrs. Hokstra. Eddy
cleared his throat.

"Yes?" his teacher asked.

"I . . . um . . . I have something to tell you."

"What is it, Eddy?"

Eddy stared down at his toes. He could hardly believe
what he was about to say. After all, this was Eddy
Thompson, for crying out loud.

"There's something about your last test that I took."

"Yes, Eddy. You did very well on the test."

"I know, only, I . . . well . . . this is so hard."

"Take all the time you need."

"I did something."

"Would you like to tell me about it?"

"No, not really. But I have to."

"Well, what is it?"

Eddy's entire body started to sweat, even behind his knees. He felt hotter than when he had been dressed in all his heavy winter clothes up in Michigan. He tried to look at his teacher, but he couldn't.

"The night before the test, I went to your house."

Mrs. Hokstra waited for him to continue.

"I went into the trash behind your apartment and I found these." He reached into his pocket and held out three crumpled papers.

Right away his teacher knew what they were. "Edward, do you know how serious this is?"

"I think so."

"You didn't *have* to come and tell me."

"Well . . . yes I did. See, something happened to me over Christmas break. I'm not the same guy I was."

"I don't understand," his teacher said.

Eddy felt a little more confident. He slowly looked up into his teacher eyes. "I've got a lot to learn about it, too. But I know I'm going to do things different."

A soft smile came over his teacher's face. "Do you know something?"

Eddy slowly shook his head.

"I'm going to retire before too long. In all the years I've been teaching, no one has ever, ever done anything like this."

"You mean you think I'm the only one who ever cheated? Because I know of lots of kids who've . . ."

"No. I mean no one has ever come in and told me the truth . . . told me they cheated. I don't know what to say."

"Well, I was wondering something."

Mrs. Hokstra reached up with her embroidered handkerchief and wiped the tears from her wrinkled cheeks. For a moment she was unable to speak.

"I was wondering," Eddy continued, "if I could study real hard and take the test over."

His teacher thought for a moment. "Hmmm."

"Could I do that?"

"Under the circumstances, and since you came to me first instead of me catching you . . . sure. Why not?"

"But there's one more problem."

"Oh?" she asked.

"I don't think there is any possible way for me to get an A on the test. And if I don't, I might not pass your history class by the end of this year."

"What did you have in mind?"

"Could I do a project for extra credit?"

She thought for a few moments. "I think that would be a fine idea. Now let me see. What should it be?"

"I thought about doing a report."

"What would it be about?"

Eddy laughed nervously. "About eight pages."

Now his teacher started to laugh. It was the first time he'd ever seen her do that.

"Actually," Eddy continued. "I'd like to do a report about John Dillenger."

"But he was such an evil person."

"I know. He used to be my hero."

"Eddy!"

"But I thought I could write about the bad things he did . . . how he made the wrong choices. Something like that."

"I think that's a wonderful idea."

"Thank you, Mrs. Hokstra. Thank you so much."

Eddy turned to leave when his teacher said, "God bless you, Edward."

He stopped, turned around, and looked back at her. Eddy saw the most beautiful smile on her face. He smiled back too, then dashed out of the room.

Eddy didn't stop running until he reached his house. He sensed a calm he had never felt before. For the first time he could remember he hadn't tried to cheat his way out of something.

When he walked in the door, his father waited for him in the kitchen. "Call Chet and Rusty. Ask them to come over. I have something to tell you."

As soon as the boys came in, Eddy took them to the den.

His father began pacing back and forth in front of the fireplace. "I have some news for you, except I'm not sure it's what you were expecting."

"What news?" Eddy asked.

"I was on the phone today with the insurance company concerning the bank money."

"And?" the boys asked.

"It isn't exactly as big a reward as you were planning on."

"How much is it?" Rusty asked.

"They're sending a thousand dollars for each of you."

"What a crummy break," Rusty whined.

"It's better than nothing," Chet told him.

"Yeah, but. . . ."

"Dad," Eddy began. "The money isn't all that important."

His father stopped pacing and gave Eddy the strangest look. "Since when?"

"Since. . . ."

"I'm going to call that bank and demand they have the insurance company give you boys more money," his father fumed.

"You don't need to do that."

"Honestly, Eddy. Lately I'm beginning to think they must have switched babies on us at the hospital."

"No, Dad. Really. I found out something while we were up at the cabin. . . . Something that's worth a lot more than money."

Eddy's father slumped into his favorite chair. All he could do was slowly shake his head. "Sometimes I wonder," he sighed.

"In a couple days, I'd like to tell you all about it."

"Please do."

Eddy's face brightened. "Do we really get to go to the cabin together every winter from now on?"

"I'd like that," his father answered.

"You mean it?" Chet asked.

"Uh huh."

Rusty looked over to Eddy. "Have you already forgotten what happened up at that place?"

A small grin turned to a broad smile on Eddy's face as he turned to Chet. "I'll never forget," Eddy said. "Best thing that ever happened to me."

- THE END -

Other Tweener Books available from Baker Trittin Concepts

Tweener Press Adventure Series

by Max Elliot Anderson

NEWSPAPER CAPER - Tom Stevens was a super sales-man. He and his friends delivered newspapers early every morning. Along their route, the boys often saw some pretty strange things. Then one day they actually became the story in their newspapers. Readers will like the humor, attack dogs, car thieves, and the chop shop Tom and his friends uncover. This story reminds us of how important friend-ship is. It also teaches that God isn't just for emergencies. He wants to guide our lives every day. - **September 2003**

NORTH WOODS POACHERS - The Washburn families have been coming to the same cabins, on the same lake, catch-ing the same fish for about as long as Andy can remember. And he's sick of it. This summer would be different, he de-cided. Only, he never imagined how different. The story is filled with excitement, danger, humor, and drama. In the end, Andy learns the concepts of family tradition, that God loves justice while He hates injustice, and that it is impor-tant to follow the rules. Readers will enjoy the gigantic jet-powered floatplane, computers, home made radio transmit-ter. and naturally, no one will ever forget Big Wall. He's a fish, of course. - **January 2004**

Other books in the series to be released in 2004:
> **MOUNTAIN CABIN MYSTERY**
> **THE SECRET OF ABBOTT'S CAVE**
> **BIG-RIG RUSTLERS**
> **LOST ISLAND SMUGGLERS**
> **RECKLESS RUNAWAY**

**Innovative Christian Publications introduces the
Gospel Storyteller Series
by Dr. Marvin G. Baker**

This series is the "Greatest Story" ever told presented in a conversational story style. It is easily read, clearly understood and enhanced with contemporary illustrations designed to encourage the reader to imagine the "story" taking place in their own neighborhood today. Each book in the five book series serves as an introduction to one of the Gospels or the Book of Acts.

**MARK'S STORY, An Introduction to the
Gospel of Mark - July 2003
MATTHEW'S STORY, An Introduction to the
Gospel of Matthew - December 2003**

The remaining books will be released in 2004.
LUKE'S STORY (the Gospel of Luke)
JOHN'S STORY (the Gospel of John)
CHURCH'S STORY (the Book of Acts)

MAX ELLIOT ANDERSON

Max Elliot Anderson is a reluctant reader even though he grew up surrounded by books. In fact, his father has written more than 70 books. In spite of his attitude toward reading, he went on to graduate from college with a degree in psychology.

In an effort to determine why he didn't like to read, he discovered that for him the style of most children's books ". . . was boring, the dialog sometimes sparse, or when it was used, it seemed to adult." He set out to write books he would like to read . . . concise books with action, suspense, and humor. His adventure series ". . . is not where all these fantastic things that couldn't possibly happen to any *one* of us, happens to the same kids, in the same town, over and over again. My books all have completely different characters, settings, and adventures."

Mr. Anderson is a Vietnam era veteran of the U.S. Army. Professionally, he has been involved in some of the most successful Christian films for children. His video productions earned many national awards, including 3 Telly Awards (the equivalent of an Oscar). He was involved in a PBS television production that received an Emmy nomination and the double album won a Grammy.

He is 56 years old, married with two adult children. He can be reached at: PO Box 4126, Rockford, IL 61110
Email Mander8813@aol.com

Order Information

If your favorite bookstore does not have *Terror at Wolf Lake* in stock, you can order it directly from the publisher for $10.95 plus $3.50 for shipping and handling per book. If five or more copies are ordered, send only $2.00 shipping and handling per book. Michigan residents add 6% sales tax.

Call 1-888-741-4386 to order today!

or

Please send ____ copies of *Terror at Wolf Lake* @ $10.95 ea.   _____
Michigan redidents please add 6% sales tax ($.66 per book) _____
Shipping and handling @ $3.50 per book   _____
    ($2.00 per book for five or more)

TOTAL _____

PLEASE PRINT

Name _____

Address _____

City _____ State _____ Zip _____

Phone _____ email _____

Credit Card # _____ Exp _____

Name on Card _____

Signature _____

Mail order blank with check or money order payable to Tweener Press
Baker Trittin Concepts, P.O. Box 20, Grand Haven, MI 49417